Praise for *Growing Up on Route 66*, the first novel in this series:

"Lund presents an entertaining story of small town life - paperboys, the gentle aspects of life in a simpler time and the wonder of the people who make small towns the linchpin of America. Through the eyes of Mark Landon we find that the answers to the myriad questions of life and love aren't always easy to find."
--Bob Moore, *ROUTE 66 MAGAZINE* (Volume 9, Number 1; Winter 2001-02)

"If the trials of Kevin, Paul, and Winnie on the television show *The Wonder Years* remind you of your childhood, you'll enjoy this coming-of-age book. The author grew up in Rolla, and his characters, Mark Landon and Marcia Terrell, live in a small Missouri town along Route 66. The narrator tells funny stories of adolescence in the 1950s. As an adult, the narrator has a philosophical outlook. 'The road I've traveled has clearer landmarks when I look behind me than when I was moving forward.'"
--Tricia Mosser, *MISSOURI LIFE* (Volume 29, Number 6; December 2001)

Praise for *Route 66 Kids*, Lund's second novel:

"Babyboomers coming of age in a small Midwestern town on Route 66. It's a decade later but it reads like the 'Summer of '42.' An extremely heartwarming and nostalgic look at young people's angst during this age of wonder."

ROUTE 66 FEDERATION NEWS (Volume 9, Number 2; Spring, 2003)

"*Route 66 Kids*, follows the fortunes of his earlier hero and heroine of *Growing up on Route 66* , Mark Landon and Marcia Terrell, taking them through high school to the eve of Mark's departure for college at Southwest Missouri State College and Marcia's departure for . . . but you'll have to read the book to find out where Marcia is headed. . . . . No matter how often you've heard the phrase/title *You Can't Go Home Again*, Michael Lund's book convinces us that Thomas Wolfe was wrong. You can go home again, and *Route 66 Kids* takes us home wherever home was."

--William Frank, *FARMVILLE (VA) HERALD*, May 31, 2002,

Praise for *A Left-Hander on Route 66* Lund's third Novel:

"[Lund's] readers are in for a surprise if not a shock, or series of shocks. In conscious and mock imitation of the opening lines of Mark Twain's *Huck Finn* . . . Lund introduces us to another struggling teen of Fairfield, Hugh Noone--read 'no one.'... *A Left-hander on Route 66* is an entertaining, interesting, highly readable autobiography of a young boy. . . "

--William Frank, FARMVILLE (VA) HERALD, Sept. 17,2003

"[*Left-hander*] is a howl with just enough of the serious to add contrast and spice."

--William Hoffman, award-winning author of *Godfires, Tidewater Blood*, and many more

Praise for *Miss Route 66* Lund's fourth Novel:

"'[W]hen do the girls get a book?' Well, here it is! *Miss Route 66* is the story . . . of Susan Bell (now Mrs. Susan Bell Thornton) of the famous Fairfield Circle and her foray into the teen-age world of beauty pageants, necking sessions, dating in the quaint world of the 50s and 60s when a girl waited for the phone to ring and didn't dare call a boy on her own."

--William Frank, *Farmville (VA) Herald*, February 18, 2004.

wandered, with curious roadside attractions and shady stops along the way. Reading [his] book is like returning to a summer night when you were young, when life was full of promise, mystery, and terror, that time at twilight, before your mother called you in to wash up and go to bed, when you were playing a leisurely game of kick-the-can and wished that the game could just go on and on. Fortunately, Lund promises that it will go on, in the second book in his series, *Route 66 Kids*, and, I hope, many more to come."

--*Eric Kraft, author of The Personal History, Adventures, Experiences & Observations of Peter Leroy*

Route 66 to Vietnam
A Draftee's Story

By
Michael Lund

BeachHouse Books

Chesterfield, Missouri, USA

Copyright

Graphics Credits:

Vietnam cover photo by Bernard Edelman. Cover design and graphics by John Lund.
First publication date November, 2004
ISBN 1-59630-000-0 Regular print BeachHouse Books Edition
ISBN 1-59630-001-9 large print (16pt) MacroPrintBooks Edition
ISBN 978159630309 ebook Kindle edition (2008)
ISBN 9781596300415 ebook edition (Mac and PC) (2008)
Library of Congress Cataloging-in-Publication Data
Lund, Michael, 1945-
    Route 66 to Vietnam : a draftee's story / by Michael Lund.
        p. cm.
    ISBN 1-59630-000-0 (alk. paper)
  1. Vietnamese Conflict, 1961-1975--Fiction. 2. United States Highway 66--Fiction. 3. Americans--Vietnam--Fiction. 4. Young men--Fiction. I. Title.
    PS3562.U486R684 2005
    813'.54--dc22

                                          2005010197

BeachHouse Books
PO Box 7151
Chesterfield, MO 63006-7151
(636) 394-4950
www.beachhousebooks.com

Route 66 to Vietnam

Michael Lund

For Stephen H. Warner
(1946-1971),

and all who served.

ACKNOWLEDGMENTS

I wish to thank these fellow Vietnam Veterans for reading this book in manuscript and offering many helpful suggestions: Neal Cronin, Bernard Edelman, Geoff Orth, Larry Parks. Bernie Edelman has offered special encouragement from the beginning to the end of this sometimes difficult undertaking.

I learned much about combat engineering from Lawrence M. Greenberg's "Jungle Eaters & Rome Plow Companies," originally published in the magazine "VIETNAM" February 1991, May 12 2000, and from the page (part of Military.com) Maintained By Bill Kimbrell

http://www.military.com/HomePage/Un itCreatedPage/0,11003,701430,00.html

Jim Shifflett edited and proofread the final manuscript, and his precision and care are greatly appreciated. Once more I must express my gratitude to Dr. Bud Banis for his ongoing support of my writing and for the larger mission he has undertaken with Science & Humanities Press.

As always, any errors in fact or inconsistencies of narration in the pages that follow are attributable solely to the author.

Prologue: Love at the Coral Court Motel

At the time I opened the closet (literally) of my Vietnam experience, I was living no more than a mile from the Coral Court Motel, famous St. Louis landmark on legendary Route 66. A night of lovemaking at that establishment coupled (if that's the right word) a war now considered disastrous for our nation with a symbol of American achievement, "The Mother Road." Strange bedfellows!

Since 1942, the Coral Court had been a comfortable stopping point for country crossing-travelers who entered the Show Me State from the east via the Chain of Rocks Bridge and then skirted the city's western edge. (This was more than twenty years before the Gateway Arch became the city's most celebrated structure.)

To unmarried or adulterous local couples, the Coral Court's attached garages had offered discrete entrances. And the unusual architecture (glass block windows, glazed beige tile, rounded corners) provided in the conservative Midwest an exotic structure appropriate for unconventional activities.

1

I proposed something like illicit behavior at the Coral Court to my wife Bella one fall in the mid 1980s, unaware that, at about the same time, my Southeast Asia past was stirring in the deepest recesses of my memory.

"You can wear something racy," I told her as we sat after dinner in our dining room. While not herself a Missourian, Bella knew of the motel's sleazy--and therefore oddly enticing--reputation. When I said "something racy," by the way, I meant garter belt and stockings, to me an erotic outfit. To her this was an uncomfortable combination she had discarded for panty hose at the earliest opportunity.

"And you?" she asked.

Me? I thought I was desirable enough in my usual boxers and T-shirt. But this got me thinking: how would I look, say, in samurai dress or as lord of the manor seducing the farmer's daughter? Perhaps I should also suggest elaborate role playing, always with me the stern disciplinarian.

The idea, of course, was that the Coral Court was the place to put the zing back in lovemaking at a time when our life ran so smoothly it threatened us with boredom. Our children were moving steadily toward high school graduation, our jobs were secure, our places in the community solid. When Bella herself made a Friday reservation at the Coral Court (both kids had planned overnights with friends), I decided she must have an idea of her own. And I was excited, despite not knowing precisely what she had in mind.

Even in a successful marriage, of course, there is never complete understanding on most matters. I've frequently entertained the illusion that my life followed a straight course once I, a college graduate, won Bella's hand, was hired by the Missouri Department of Transportation, and fathered my first child. And I thought I drove us all down that road. Arabella Landon née Wilfer, however, not only had a hand on the wheel, but often decided the route I thought I was selecting.

And there's more, I now know, that determines our path in life. Immovable objects are always out there in front and to the side of us, blocking our way and sometimes knocking us off course. At some times these barriers are of such massive size they allow us only one route into the future. Vietnam was that kind of unavoidable obstacle for me, as well as for other young men of Fairfield, like Billy Rhodes, Larry Thornton, and Howie Bend.

The Coral Court Motel a decade and a half later, however, represented a happy straying from the straight and narrow, a detour from steady advance toward what I'd begun to fear, some sort of mid-life crisis.Ironically, it turned out that my Vietnam experience did more to carry me through this difficult passage than would new ventures in eroticism.

There had been talk that the Coral Court might be torn down, another price paid to the American theme of growth and development. Still, more and more citizens from Chicago to Los Angeles were beginning to call for the restoration and preservation of "America's Main Street."

Personally, I was of two minds about this. I believed in growth and prosperity, but I also didn't want to lose contact with central values in our tradition. When the Coral Court Motel got mixed up with the Vietnam War in my mind, I didn't know which, if either, I should leave behind.

Ninety-five percent of my experience in Vietnam, I believed, was, at least on the surface, either banal or comic. Unfortunately, the remaining five percent was especially tragic. For fifteen years all I could see was the tragic part. So I buried it deep from public view and private contemplation.

4

Then, a series of chance occurrences brought my overseas experience to the surface. Reluctantly, I came to the conclusion that this return to the past was probably unavoidable, and perhaps necessary. I'll begin that journey proper in the next chapter when two Phyllises come to my front door.

However, I wouldn't have expected a trip through such memories to be pleasant, as I had originally hoped a return to the Coral Court would be. I had taken Bella there once before, when I was on orders for Vietnam and she was starting graduate work in psychology at St. Louis University. I thought she'd give herself to me in the same spirit I believed World War II brides-to-be had treated their soldiers going off to war. If they might never return, shouldn't they get want they wanted on the eve of battle?

I assumed I would take her gift, having turned a bit cynical as the draft pursued me and my friends at Southwest Missouri State College down in Springfield. Although not a virgin, I'd still had only a limited number of sexual encounters and thought the world that was going to send me to war owed me something more. But things didn't turn out the way I anticipated with Bella.

In part that was good. It seems we refrained because in the end I knew that this was the woman I wanted to bear my children. And that's not what I would have been about in my first time at the Coral Court. But it was bad in that, despite the generous offer she made, I failed physically to respond.

"We could be young again," Bella said somewhat wistfully in contemplating a second try at the Coral Court. Neither of us alluded to the details of that earlier time in the motel or the context of my going overseas. I was being offered a rewrite of that difficult night nearly twenty years later, not a reenactment. Surely I would succeed this time. Whatever spice Bella contemplated adding to our regular lovemaking would only guarantee the necessary excitement.

She began with the customary "I guess I should slip into something more comfortable." We'd had dinner at a nearby restaurant and contemplated only briefly finding somewhere we might dance. The week had been hectic enough even before the hurry of today, and we were tired. I'd had a late meeting about property acquisition on my current project. And she had to ferry Nelson to choir practice and Jenny to soccer before they ate, packed, and were dropped off at respective friends' houses.

So, I lay on the bed watching an old movie on TV--wasn't this the Warner

Brothers' 1953 *Kiss Me Kate* with Kathryn Grayson?   And I reminded myself of one sweet advantage to being married to a psychologist: Bella knew what I liked. Images of the Sheik of Araby throwing a veiled woman over the shoulders of his horse and riding off into the desert floated through my mind.

Of course, sometimes Bella also decided what I *should* like rather than what I wanted and marched straight ahead on the basis of her own recognizance. I heard rustling behind the bathroom door, the unzipping of the overnight bag she'd taken with her.

The room we were in was not exactly the same as the one we'd stayed in years ago. It had an extra rounded bay in the front with a Murphy bed, which, of course, we didn't need. And the main room had a pyramid shaped, glass block window on its rounded corner, one more unusual and intriguing feature.

I had been unable to think of a good outfit to hide in my overnight bag, so I went with the old standard: the birthday suit. "No secrets here!" I'd imagined myself saying when she unveiled whatever surprise she had for me. I was, of course, keeping more of me hidden than I realized at the time.

I'd always insisted I was another Midwestern "open book," the surface matching the depths, outside same as inside. But when Bella stepped out of the Coral Court's bathroom, the shock reminded me that my life had actually been a bit more complicated.

She was wearing, as I had hoped, a garter belt (provocatively black) and sheer stockings. But above that she had on my old Army field jacket, the Vietnam service medal pinned above the pocket. What initial confusion stemmed from her appearance is to be told in the pages that follow. But, I have since come to believe that the healing of the deepest psychological scars in my adult life began with this single dramatic moment.

Mark Landon

St. Louis, Missouri

Volume One: The Dog of War. Chapter I.

A week after our return to the Coral Court, I was not really surprised by the unexpected visit of the two Phyllises. It was the second in a series I recognized as memory-sparking events.

Taz--I called him our "terrible terrier"--raced barking through the living room at the first sound of the doorbell. I had just gotten home from the dentist, worried about an off-again, on-again toothache he said didn't require immediate treatment.

Taz blocked me at the foot of the stairs, snarling and spinning in the foyer. So, as usual, I gave up trying to get past him and went out the kitchen door through the garage. I came to the front porch on our own sidewalk from the driveway.

"Hello. Sorry about the dog," I said to the two middle-aged women--one Asian, one white--standing three steps above me. I suspected that they were religious fundamentalists and was relieved to realize they couldn't block my retreat back inside the house. "He's terrible," I apologized, gesturing toward the door, behind which Taz kept up a steady, vicious barking.

"Now, sir, don't you apologize for that dog," said the Asian woman. "That's the best friend you can have in times like these."

Her companion nodded. She was older and dumpy, her face drawn in where teeth were probably missing. A pale blue sweater showed wear, while the other woman wore a neat, dark suit, a deep maroon blouse. Both were holding Bibles.

"We're two Phyllises," explained the first woman, smiling, and reached out a hand. She gave their last names, but I lost them in amusement at this practiced delivery, 'the two Phyllises.' "We're here to say you need a dog like this, the world being what it is." I shook her hand, putting one foot up on the bottom step.

"Um-hmm," confirmed Phyllis the Second. I shook her hand also, but turned back to look at the first Phyllis, a strikingly beautiful woman. Her hair, jet black, hung down behind her back.

"Well, still . . . "

"The way this world is these days," resumed the speaking Phyllis, "there isn't any good news. Do you watch your television in the evening?"

"Some days." She held her Bible close to her breast.

"There used to be good news on the radio, but not any longer. All you see is terrible--murder, robbery, deadly diseases--right?" ("Hmm-um," from the shadow Phyllis.) "When I was growing up--I'm from Malaysia--when I was young, there used to be good news. Do you know what I mean?"

"Yes, I guess I do." Could I hear faint echoes of a British accent in her speech?

"I remember listening to the radio with my mother, the Queen's coronation. That was a happy day."

"Yes." I had no real idea who was queen--Elizabeth?--or when this would have been--the '50s?

"Oh, yes, that was good news. But now all you see on TV is death, and rape, and killing, and assault. Isn't that so?"

The other Phyllis nodded again. I shrugged, beginning to feel it was time to end this conversation. With my tongue I tested my tooth for pain. Was that toothache coming back?

"Now, there's good news here," the Asian Phyllis concluded, holding the Bible still more tightly. "Yes, this is good news."

"Well, yes. I know about that. And I've talked before with . . . with you people. But we're pretty happy with our church life right now." We had not been to church in weeks.

"Well, good, wonderful," smiled the woman from Malaysia. The other Phyllis nodded her satisfaction. I didn't even have to take any of their literature. But I agreed to keep that dog, anyone's best friend in these times. I waved goodbye.

Later, after dinner, I went upstairs for a sweater and nearly stepped on Taz sniffing at the closet door. Getting in my way seemed to be his mission today.

"Oh, come on!" I said and swung the door open to show him there was nothing there. I pointed to shoe boxes full of photographs I had never bothered to sort or put in albums. Costumes for the children's Halloween and school plays were also crammed into bags or hung next to out-of-style suits and dresses from the '60s. Extra packing material--foam pads, boxes of styrofoam peanuts and excelsior--had been stuffed on the shelf.

As these things appeared through the doorway, a sharp stab of pain registered itself in my tooth.

"Ow!" I said out loud, putting a hand to my jaw almost as if I'd been shot. That tooth was hurting!

"Taz, who had slipped through the door and was snarling at one of the shoe boxes on the floor.

I could see that this box had cassette tapes in it, probably music recorded from albums years ago. Where the side of the box had sagged with age I could see a row of tape boxes. One had an odd look, and something prompted me to take off the top.

Taz barked and scooted past me into the hall. I pulled out the one tape and stood up. What was this?

The rectangular plastic box had an address label glued to the flat surface. It was directed to me at my parents' home in Fairfield with the return address, "APO SF." It had been mailed from Vietnam. I realized this from the address (Army Post Office, San Francisco) and the fact that it had no postage, just the word "FREE" written in one corner.

I recalled who had sent the tape: Anthony Roberts, a man I'd served with in the Army Corps of Engineers, a man who died when a mortar shell exploded in our compound three weeks after I had left for the States, one week before his D.E.R.O.S. ("Date Eligible for Return from Overseas"). This was not a music tape, but an audio letter sent from a "short-timer" to someone who had just returned to "the World."

I had played the tape only once, when I first received it. Later, word of Anthony's death, as well as a desire to put Vietnam behind me, must have kept the tape hidden in dark storage spots like the hall closet. It was not, I know now, just Anthony's death that I kept hidden.

Anthony had recorded his letter on a portable recorder bought on R&R in Hong Kong. With popular songs ("We Gotta Get Out of This Place") interspersed, he filled his buddy in on what was happening in "the Nam." I remembered that Tony's voice had been hard to listen to the first time.

I recalled more: in kidding his stateside buddy about what he was missing, Anthony had probably mentioned one famous night of guard duty. We had been on alert after rumors of sappers came through HQ. But I had walked to the bunker at midnight, high from half a dozen Falstaffs, my drug of choice at the time. I'd been in-country for months

14

and was beginning to wonder if I'd ever go home.

At 0200 hours the field phones went dead. I had the receiver to my ear and was cranking the handle furiously, trying to raise anyone. Then, when the floodlights went out, and a nervous tower guard opened up on the perimeter with his machine-gun, I joined in with an M-16. Something was moving in the barbed wire.

Flares revealed that the area was quiet. A patrol later found the body of a dog, shot cleanly through the heart. Although no one knew if the tower guard or I had fired the fatal round, the rest of company called me "Gunner" for months and responded to any anxiety with the refrain: "Beware the dog of war!"

With a little shiver, I put the tape back in the box. I kept my hand on the doorknob for a moment, however, hesitating. Then I took out the tape again and went downstairs. In the living room I switched on the stereo, dropped in the tape. Settling in an easy chair, I put on a set of expensive earphones.

There might, I realized, be other things on the tape I had not at first remembered. I had a hazy recollection of a weekend in Saigon, for instance, with a woman (we'd called them all "girls") named Sue. (How did I get there? Frankly, I didn't remember.) And hadn't there been some quasi-illegal money exchange scheme I had participated in with Tony?

Again I paused, a finger on the "PLAY" button. Should I listen? This could resurrect things better left forgotten. On the other hand, I might be at the stage in life where I could let out the skeletons. Still, the pretty Phyllis had insisted these were dangerous times. Should I stop here, avoid returning to a troublesome past? "Beware," I whispered aloud, "the dog of war."

But perhaps there was nothing startling on the tape after all. Not even a reference to that infamous night on the perimeter. The voice letter might include only superficial talk, all the old clichés from Army life: how many days everyone had left, what it would be like to live as a civilian again, sentimental (and often ironic) mooning for a bright future, romantic hopes.

"Ow!" I cried, and my hand went to the side of my jaw. My finger pushed the button. I had gone ahead.

II

"It's dead," my dentist Bill had told me, holding up his hands in their sallow rubber gloves. This was earlier in the same day the two Phyllises came to visit.

"Dead?" I repeated. I was slumped back in the chair.

"Dead," confirmed Bill. "Probably the result of trauma, perhaps long ago. Have you ever been hit on that side of the jaw? Did you run into a brick wall sometime?"

"Well, let's see . . . " All those cables and cords, visible over his shoulder, were distracting me. They connected, I guessed, the different pieces of equipment.

"Or an infection, sometimes spreading from the ear can do it." Hoses for air and water provided a soft background of hiss and hum to this explanation.

"I don't remember . . . " The long arm of the drill, bent in the shape of a praying mantis, loomed behind Bill. I was having trouble thinking, hemmed in by equipment.

"Even wearing braces when you were a teenager. Severe or too rapid dislocation can cut off the blood supply. It will go without your knowing it."

"You mean my tooth may have died twenty years ago, thirty-five years ago?" I struggled to sit more upright. These damned dentist chairs--they're designed to keep you locked in humiliating positions. I couldn't get out without a struggle.

"That's right," continued Bill. He held the X-ray up to the light again, studying it. "The tooth is there, but not living tissue anymore. It's really just taking up space."

He pulled down the mask covering the lower half of his face and turned away to snap off his rubber gloves. Of course! AIDS, latest threat to a long life, had inspired this extra precaution.

I twisted in the chair to keep visual contact as he washed his hands at a little sink by the door. "And I never had any sign? I went on as if everything was fine?"

"Sure. That's not uncommon. The tooth was functional; you didn't feel anything especially different. Until recently." I noticed that Bill must have cut himself shaving that morning, a little nick just down from his left ear. Hmm. Whose blood are we afraid of here? Yet another crisis of the modern age.

"I never felt any pain, though." I wasn't being completely honest. When the tooth had bothered me, I had taken the rest of an old antibiotic prescribed for Bella's chronic bronchitis.

"Still, that occasional tenderness, a sensitivity to cold, is a sign we may need to pull it. Or do a root canal." Bill touched with a fingertip the scratch beneath his own ear.

"Well, root canal, whatever. Let's get it over with." I'd first gone to Bill just because he was in our church and I knew him. But I'd come to like him. He was slow, precise.

"Oh, no. It takes several sessions. And, from what you say, it's not urgent, even though there was probably an infection. It's not causing you pain now, right?" Bill stepped on a pedal, and the chair sank down to a normal level. Another pedal, and the back cranked up so that I was returned at last to a sitting posture. But my underwear had ridden up uncomfortably.

"Not right now anyway. The soreness I was telling you about, that was some weeks ago. I mainly came in for my regular checkup." The way he stood was blocking me from getting up.

"You could go months or years, then." He penciled a note on my chart and turned to make a summary: "The tooth is just there right now, doing its job, more or less. You're lucky it isn't discolored. But one day--perhaps when you're a bit run down from a virus--or during a time of stress, say--it'll start acting up. You should let me know if the pain really kicks in, or if there is any swelling." He unhooked the little chain that held the paper bib under my chin, pulling up the armrest so that, at last, I could step out of the chair. "Let's see you in, ah, six months?"

Driving out of the parking lot, I released a sigh of relief: I was free! Though I generally preferred to get unpleasant things taken care of right away, I had to feel some pleasure that drilling was not going to be a part of this day.

Still, what had Bill said? A time of stress, that might be it. Could I be feeling some pressure at home and at work I wasn't fully aware of? I hadn't admitted to Bill that the tooth hurt more, and more often, than I'd said.

I swerved suddenly into the middle lane so I could cross over to the McDonald's. I would celebrate escaping the (dentist's) chair by having something to eat with my dead tooth.

One car away from McDonald's large menu sign and intercom, I reviewed the options years of stopping with two children had made familiar to me. When I pulled forward, a sweet, teenager's voice asked, "Can I take your order?" My invisible waitress was around the corner, I knew, punching in drive-through requests on her computer/cash register.

"Let me have a danish and a large coffee."

She would be wearing a headset, gray band across the top of her head. One ear would be open, the other holding an earphone the size of a quarter. A thin wire frame held a microphone in front of her lips. This particular system worked well, none of that crackle or static that made communication difficult.

"Would you like some french fries with your order?" I knew the hard sell, pleasant but persistent.

"No, thank you."

"Orange juice?"

"Not today."

"Cream or sugar for that coffee?"

She had exactly the cheerfulness of a McDonald's waitress on television commercials. She was programmed to stop me long enough to find out all my needs and inspire new desires.

"One cream, two sugars." I imagined a petite teenage blonde, hair pulled back in a ponytail, ringing up the total and calling to her youthful associates for help with the order. She would pour the coffee. I eased around the corner and toward the little window where she stood in her glass cage.

The McDonald's girl was exactly as I had pictured her. Her ponytail bounced as she leaned out to take my money. When she turned to the register, I saw the battery pack riding in the small of her back, giving her mobility even as she took and put together orders. A thin cable ran up to her neck.

I pulled out of McDonald's, having smiled politely at "Debbie" (I'd read her blue name tag) as she handed me a cup and a paper bag marked by yellow arches. Through the headset, connected to the hip-riding battery pack, she was asking the next customer for an order even as she smiled farewell to me.

On Lindbergh, cruising in late morning traffic, I contemplated this picture of Debbie McDonald's. I saw her tight, short skirt, the white blouse tucked in neatly. The gray cloth

22

belt that held her battery pack, which had been eye-level to me in the seat of the car, accented the flat stomach of youth.

Marriage had been good to me, though in the last few years, as I've said, our life--even our love life--had fallen into uneventful routine. Like any man, I tried to blame it on my wife. Hence, the Coral Court.

There were no problems at work, unless you counted the goofy Banisters, whose property lay in the path of the road I had to build. But I'd faced similar difficulties in my work before and knew that patience, fairness, and, of course, the state's eminent domain always won out.

Bella's erotic role-playing as an Army specialist seducing a virgin recruit had not evoked unsettling memories from my months in Vietnam, or so I thought at the time. Mostly we laughed and got excited. (If you'll forgive the crude military slang here, you could accurately say I had "re-upped.")

I didn't think we'd do too much dressing in costumes for lovemaking in the future. But deliberately taking a break from routine appealed to both of us. It didn't occur to me to ask until some days later if Bella's wearing my old uniform was an expression of her own desire to return to a past event.

23

She had waited faithfully for me during my year overseas, finishing the first two semesters of her graduate program. Her weekly letters told me of classes taken, books read, papers and projects completed. There was nothing, really, of her own struggle concerning the most divisive war in U.S. history. And, stupidly, I'd never asked.

I understood that many college students opposed the war, and my own enthusiasm for the conflict was lukewarm at best. But as long as my college student deferment had lasted, I'd been able to avoid thinking too hard about our nation's policies. When my "greetings" from Uncle Sam came a few weeks after graduation, I did what my father's generation had done: swore the oath of allegiance and hoped to be strong enough to do my duty as a good American. To this day, I can't say whether I did or not.

III.

Driving home on the afternoon of my dentist appointment--before the two Phyllises were to show up on my doorstep--I witnessed an accident. No one was hurt, but the event added to my sense that the fabric of the past was unraveling.

Several blocks from my house I spotted a bright flash in the corner of my eye. Turning my head quickly, I saw a man in a flamboyant orange jumpsuit clearing his lawn of debris. Armed with a blower that looked like a giant hair dryer, he drove a wall of brown oak and maple leaves down a long slope to the gutter.

The leaf blower was orange like the man's work clothes, which, looking closer, I realized were at least two sizes too large for him. An orange extension cord trailing back to the long porch of the brick rancher made him look like an astronaut linked to his space station. He wore goggles to protect his eyes and a red St. Louis Cardinals baseball cap turned backwards. When he shook out his lifeline to keep it free of tangles, he resembled someone on a space walk, tethered to the mother ship.

Just as I pulled even with the man, I saw him retreat one step from the leaf pile, catch his heel on an uneven spot in the lawn, and roll onto his back. It looked as if someone had jerked his lifeline, perhaps giving him a signal, but too energetically.

I flinched in sympathy, afraid all of a sudden that my tooth was about to resume hurting. But I was relieved to see the man immediately roll forward onto his feet again. He went down so fast and popped back up so easily, it looked like a cartoon accident. Orange Man, I thought. Nothing can hurt him!

Still, I braked to a stop, my way blocked by the image of his falling. I rolled down the window and called to him, "You okay?"

"Yes," laughed invulnerable Orange Man. "No problem."

He raised a hand, waving me off. I drove on, but the experience stuck with me. The blower's electric cord running back to the house now reminded me of airmen I had seen in Vietnam.

Loading or off-loading, Huey door gunners stood watchfully beside their birds, huge blades rotating at reduced speed above them. The men were plugged into the chopper's communication system by cables connected to headsets in their helmets. And (like Debbie at McDonald's) they spoke to the rest of the crew through tiny microphones mounted before their lips on little wire frames.

The man in the oversized orange uniform also recalled the figure of Bella in my olive-drab Army uniform at the Coral Court a week earlier. The sharp image of Orange Man's falling and these cloudy pictures from my military past were creating an undercurrent of anxiety.

I think of myself as a prudent man. And it may be that I have at times been overly cautious, nursing an exaggerated fear of future accidents. Our two-story house has twice the recommended number of smoke detectors. I tend to replace all the hoses in both family cars every three years, regardless of mileage. In general, my doctor cannot recommend a diagnostic test I won't take. Hoping never to need dental work again (how vain that hope is!), I brush and floss ferociously.

I have also prepared relentlessly for the demands of the future, anticipating ways around tomorrow's obstacles. When I find a comfortable style of shoe, I sometimes buy two or three pair, fearing the company may stop making them. I put the spares in the closet for that distant time when they will be needed.

Once quartz watches became inexpensive, I purchased half a dozen Timexes in a style I found comfortable: white face, black hands, simple calendar, dark leather band. I should never need to shop for a watch again. And I always know the time. When the current timepiece finally breaks or is lost, I simply produce its mate and strap it to my wrist, never losing a beat.

If I like the shirt Bella gives me at Christmas, I ask her to buy several more. The extras stay folded and wrapped on my closet shelf until needed, though Bella had complained she has nothing left to shop for at birthdays and holidays. I have backup pants, reserve blue blazers, boxes of spare underwear and socks.

Bella knows several psychological terms for my obsessions, but at the time of our Coral Court adventure I rested secure in my material and method. Even such an exotic night out as that had been carefully scripted, if not correctly in some key details. Now a toothache and two Phyllises and the Orange Man and Tony Roberts' Vietnam tape were shaking the foundations of my stable world.

Even the present was not as solid as I tried to believe. The Banisters of Franklin County were exhibiting a tenacity I'd not experienced before, and they represented a major problem for me as road engineer.

Ralph and Sarah Banister owned twenty acres of land near Pacific, Missouri, across which a new stretch of Interstate 44 needed to go. I had to convince them to sell and move (at a government determined price) or find another route.

I knew there were two main problems I faced if I tried to go around the Banisters': rock and water. There was a mountain to the north of the farm and a river valley to the south. Our survey team had told me the best path by far for the highway upgrade was right through the old farmhouse of these long-term Show Me State residents. But I'd made a crucial mistake early in my discussion with Ralph and Sarah: I'd come to like them. And now I didn't want to have to make them move.

"Come in, young man!" Mr. Banister had said immediately when I introduced myself as an engineer with the Department of Transportation. "Sarah, nice young man here. Come join us."

Already past forty, I loved to be called "young," even if it was by someone I assumed was at least an octogenarian. Mrs. Banister, when she made her way slowly but deliberately into the living room, appeared to be as old as her husband.

I saw right away that they were America's archetypal grandparents: white haired, plump (though not unpleasantly so), soft-spoken, and openly kind. "Can I get you some coffee?" Sarah asked, eager to make me comfortable. "Sit, sit."

"Oh no, nothing to drink. I'm just here to gather some information for the department. We're always making plans, as I guess you know. How to handle more and more cars on the road."

They were so agreeable, both of them. I couldn't imagine not winning them over to the public's need for a better highway.

"Oh, I know what you mean about planning," Ralph said. "It's the two-car families and the commuters, not just more people."

"Of course. So, we like to take our surveys, keep track of the trends. You don't mind a few questions yourselves, do you?"

Naturally, I was doing more than gathering numbers. I would be subtly making the case for a straighter, wider Interstate path. It wouldn't be until my third or fourth visit that I would explain how the safest way to handle all this increased traffic would be a new route for the road, a route right across the middle of their property.

Late in my second visit, however, I began to discover a deeper core of self-assurance in this couple I had tagged as pliable and cooperative. They introduced me to their aging dachshund, offered coffee and pound cake, showed pictures of their vacations and their grandchildren. They were satisfied with the life they had lived, despite its hardships.

"You know," Mr. Banister observed. "You know, I'm not sure I understand your generation. Not you, of course, I don't mean you in particular."

"That's okay. I'm not sure how typical I am anyway."

"It's this 'Me Generation' I hear about. Everybody seems to want to get everything for himself--more, more, more."

"Now Ralph, the country's doing well." Sarah leaned forward in her rocker to remind me of something my own parents had insisted on: "We grew up in the Depression,

31

you know. Times were hard. But young people expect more now."

"We were happy to have just what we needed. Nowadays, why, people spend because they have the money."

"You're right, you're right," I admitted. "We all want big houses and fine cars."

Then I stopped, realizing that applying this logic too thoroughly might end up going against building bigger highways, highways that would have to take old farmhouses to handle the traffic of more fine cars.

What I also didn't learn until I got pretty far into the negotiations with the Banisters was that there was a deeper issue here than finding a route for the new section of interstate. The Banisters already knew, for instance, that one big question was what to do with old stretches of Route 66, America's Highway. And portion of their property, it turned out, included a section of the original Mother Road, abandoned by the government decades ago for the first of many "improvements."

IV.

Contemplating the chances of a tooth going bad--as mine had--I wondered about the forces that shape individual lives. Are they patterned or random? I had always viewed my experiences in Vietnam as unlikely coincidences, contradicting any notion of divine or human order. Meeting Billy Rhodes on my second day in-country had been a perfect example of the world's randomness.

Unlike the fate of Tony Roberts, it was one of the stories I was willing to tell about my year over there. (I had never told the dog story, and no additional "smoking gun" of repressed experience had emerged after I listened to his tape again.)

"Wanna' get a beer?" Billy said, as if we were back in town for a weekend. I would have come up from Springfield, he down from Columbia when we were in college.

"What!" Here I was stripped, as it were, of my civilian (my true) identity, carrying everything I owned as an Army PFC in a single duffle bag. And there in the sand path on a sprawling American military base just off the shore of the South China Sea was a guy I had grown up with, sporting jungle fatigues and a tropical tan but grinning as if we'd never been drafted. Billy Rhodes, the guy who would do anything and usually did.

"You'll be waiting here two hours at least for processing. My hootch is five minutes away. Come on." Billy was in supply, to my mind one of the cases where the Army matched ability to assignment. It's true that I was given a 12B20 M.O.S. (Military Occupational Specialty). That is, I was a "pioneer" combat engineer. But, as I'll explain at some point, you couldn't really call what I did over there "construction."

"You're sure . . . ?" I wondered, but accepted anyway the fiction that we were back in our childhood neighborhood of the Circle. Billy led me off through Cam Ranh Bay's oppressive humidity and blinding sun. And, reenacting many a childhood adventure, we lingered for more than "a" beer before he returned me to Personnel, where I hadn't been missed in the slow movement of the Army's vast support system in the rear. Still, I had eventually to resume my place in that relentless machinery.

Fretting about the Banisters' stubbornness years later, I marveled at Billy's innocent year in Vietnam. "Never heard a shot fired in anger," he always claimed, though we both knew it wasn't completely true. He counted his giant base's "outgoing" as routine, America's superior firepower targeting regions of the country, not individuals or specific operations. The enemy fire I'd heard was, I'm happy to say, a healthy enough distance away.

What would it be like to make love to Debbie McDonald's, I wondered the day after the visit of the two Phyllises, the rediscovery of Tony's tape, the first sharp recollections of Vietnam in fifteen years. Intriguing distraction!

At home after work, I was in front of the family room television set, forgetting or, more likely, deliberately pushing to the back of my mind the dentist, the Banisters, the fallen Orange Man, Billy's surprise greeting 10,000 miles from Fairfield.

Would that nymph's freshness and joy be an antidote to middle-age depression, man with a dead tooth? Would her youth take me back to my youth, before I had the burdens of maturity (marriage, mortgage, parenthood, career)? Would I be as I was before Vietnam? I began by imagining Debbie on top.

Bella was getting dinner ready. Over the counter that separated kitchen from family room, I saw her punching a code into the microwave, reheating weekend lasagna. She was still dressed from work. The children were in their rooms.

Of course Debbie would be on top: I knew I was out of shape and couldn't have controlled her or the situation. I saw her again in my mind's eye, on her knees astride me and wearing the standard McDonald's outfit. Her blonde hair, pulled loose from the ponytail, hung down across her face.

"My terminal came today," Bella called from the kitchen. She held the door to the refrigerator open, looking around it.

"Oh? Good." I held a scotch and water in one hand, resting it on one arm of my favorite easy chair. I had slipped into a mellow mood, easing the worries. "Everything hooked up right?"

Debbie was suddenly naked in my fantasy. Her modest breasts were high and firm. I could hear her making sounds, breathing heavily, calling out--what? My name? An entreaty to stop? To go on? She seemed to be biting her lip.

"They say so," Bella replied, putting plates on the counter and pointing to the table where the four of us regularly ate our meals. I should put them out, I realized. "But I didn't have time to try logging on and using programs."

In my daydream Debbie's hips were rocking. But she was light, and I could hold her. (In fact a dream girl, she was no weight at all!) I was pleased in my fantasy not to feel any climax approaching. I would wait for her.

I got up slowly from the easy chair, turned the sound on the TV down, and began putting the plates at their places. I took the silverware Bella had set on the counter and arranged it around the table. But at the same time I kept up my erotic daydream.

Debbie was moving more wildly now, not just back and forth, but side to side in an orbit of desire. And she was talking--first pleading, then making sharp, terse commands. Her hair whipped this way and then that as she swung her head from side to side. I saw her mouth wide and eyes looking into the distance. She was losing herself entirely.

I returned to my chair, took a long drink of the scotch. "It just takes time," I called out to Bella. I had been among the first to rely on the computer for my operation. And I knew there could be glitches and delays, sometimes even a total system crash.

I noticed that Debbie had something on her face, a kind of wire frame in front of her mouth. Those weren't her glasses falling down, where they? (Had she worn glasses?) It couldn't be a night guard prescribed to a young person by an ancient orthodontist, straightening teeth? No, that wasn't it. Ah, she's still wearing her drive-through headset!

Bella came around the counter and stood with one hand on the back of my chair, looking at the silent TV. "Can you come over this weekend? Just run through the system once with me?"

I realized now that Debbie was completely calm in her relationship to me, even though my body writhed beneath her. She was more purposefully grinding away. The gray belt holding her battery pack drove forward and pulled back. That unbelievably flat stomach, rippled washboard!

"Sure. I guess. Saturday morning?"

"It's important that I find out how things work, you know. I want to be a full member of the team now." She rested a hip on the side of the chair, put an arm across my shoulders. My dream self was losing energy.

"Of course. Gotcha." I reached around and patted Bella's bottom. She'd finally secured a full-time position a month ago.

38

The busy movement in Debbie's arms and shoulders was all directed to the taking and filling of orders. She was calling out for sandwiches, pouring drinks. At the same time she talked over the intercom with new customers as they pulled up to the drive-through speaker in a long line. Into her headset she called, "Would you like some fries with that order? Was that a large or medium Sprite? Will you have your apple turnover heated?" My fantasy self wilted.

"I saw the cutest girl at McDonald's today."

"Oh?" Bella came around the side of the chair to look me in the face, blocking my view of the television.

"'Debbie,' her tag said. She seemed so bright. Wish I had her outlook. Or her prospects."

"Now don't you start looking at teenage girls or I'll have to think about getting a 'puppy.'" Back to the kitchen, she began pouring drinks and putting them up on the counter.

"A puppy? We have our dog." And a terrible dog it is, I thought.

"Not a dog, a 'puppy.' That's what I learned from a California woman at that workshop last week." She put on hot mitts to get the dish from the microwave.

I remembered vaguely her account of "Human Behavior and Contemporary Moral Issues." Bella went on. "Middle-aged men have always desired younger women, girls. Now liberated older women, at least in some parts of the country, are less inhibited about their own sexual desires."

"So, what's a 'puppy'?"

"That's it. A boy partner for a middle-aged woman, a 'puppy.'" She put the lasagna on a hot plate, carrying the steaming top back to the kitchen in her gloved hand.

Whoa! I didn't really feel I was looking for a Lolita, despite this Debbie fantasy. Surely Bella was not talking about herself? She couldn't already have a puppy, could she?

V.

Dinner went, as it so often seemed to in those benign years of my early middle age, smoothly. But while we passed the bread and praised the lasagna, I heard a faint echo of Tony Roberts' voice on tape beneath the family conversation. A second troublesome moment for "Gunner" Landon was being called up from buried memories. At the same time I felt again a familiar twinge of pain in an upper back right molar--toothache.

While Tony specifically reminded me in his audio letter to "beware the dog of war," he had not alluded directly to what we called "joint coed naked showering." But one word in his account had jiggled this erotic image loose from my decade-and-a-half's repression. He referred to Sydney, my R & R destination.

Now that I think back, it's possible Bella's reference to a different kind of "puppy" love also connected in my mind to this Vietnam memory, and to our night at the Coral Court. When she dressed (at least partially) as Specialist Mark Landon, Bella reminded me of someone. (Her aggressive behavior might also have hinted she was seeking something I hadn't been offering.)

"R & R," Rest and Recreation, was a constant subject of daydreams for the American soldier in Vietnam. From the moment we landed in-country (in my case, even before being greeted by Billy), we began planning the five days we could spend in places like Bangkok, Hawaii, Singapore, Taiwan, or Hong Kong.

Married personnel generally met their wives in Honolulu, reaffirming a life together. Sadly, though, R & R became for many couples a marital dead end, especially those who had just married and were not prepared for the strain of separation. Public protest back home brought out more and more private resentment after the Tet Offensive in 1968. And the frustration of girlfriends and wives was sometimes unfairly directed toward the men who had been asked to carry out national policy. I seem to remember at least half a dozen divorces in my unit alone.

Single troops taking R & R, on the other hand, blew whatever money they had saved from six months' service on booze and women wherever those entities were available.

A small number of enterprising men, by the way, also stuffed their return bags with discount Japanese cameras, fine watches, and miscellaneous electronic equipment available through civilian channels across the Pacific command. Others in their unit paid top dollar for these hard-to-get items and mailed them home to friends and family, or resold them on the black market.

Sydney was the tamest place for R & R debauchery, as that English-speaking country had its own troops in Vietnam and saw Americans not just as sources of cash but as allies in a global fight against Communism. Young Aussie women who'd seen their own beaus off to war were friendly to visiting GI's. I can put this another way: you didn't always have to pay for sex in Sydney.

This is certainly what Peter Ward assured me when I was on the eve of departure. He had returned several weeks earlier from his stay Down Under. "I got laid more times than days in the week," he bragged. "The women there are *soooo* sympathetic to us soldier boys from the States."

Ward's confidence about all matters irritated me, but I hoped he was right in this case.

"All you need to do, Mark," he explained, "is go to any night spot. You'll find the girls there, and they'll know you're American. Or, if you're like me, they'll find you!" He winked at the small crowd sitting around the table at the enlisted men's club. We were drinking beer at fifteen cents a can while the sound system blasted out tunes by The Who.

Ward was one of those guys who took it for granted that good fortune was no accident. Popular in high school, good if not brilliant in college, guaranteed a job through family connections in the New York State Department of Transportation, he saw life as smooth sailing. He acknowledged no obstacles in his path to prosperity, not even Vietnam.

"When they come back to the hotel with you, they'll do it, no question. What's great is getting them into the shower. You can't believe how much fun your little bar of soap can have!"

There was a round of excited laughter from men whose most recent sexual fulfillment came through thumbing worn copies of *Playboy* or ogling female singers in the Filipino rock-and-roll bands that toured major bases. Still, I did my best to believe in this attractive scenario. Decidedly less confident, however, I spent my first days touring museums, browsing in shops, waiting to be discovered by a girl who needed a man.

Now, it's true that I was semi-engaged to Bella at this time, and that may have contributed to my reserved approach. But she had insisted I was not committed to her at my return. "A year's a long time, Mark," she argued. "Let's keep writing and then see how we feel." Still, I had sworn my eternal love.

Even though I shouldn't have been so dense, it never occurred to me to worry about her feelings. Perhaps what Bella really meant was that she wanted the chance to say "no" at the end of my year's service. After all, I might not have returned the same as I left, or even returned at all.

The prevailing mentality of GI's, though, was that what we did in Vietnam was disconnected from our home identities. Sadly, I suspect this mentality contributed to excesses in the field and to questionable financial dealings in the rear. And, no less horny than all the others, I bought into this view myself in terms of sexual adventures. If I got lucky in Sydney, it didn't somehow count as a betrayal of Bella, the woman I was confident would one day bear my children.

I'd met "Cindy of Sydney" (as I later bragged of her to others in my unit) at Bondi Beach, a beautiful stretch of sand in one of the city's pleasant suburbs. There are ancient aboriginal rock engravings a short walk away, but I was more interested in the sunlit and tanned present than the dark and distant past.

Cindy was just as friendly as Peter Ward had predicted. We met at an ice cream stand, walked along the water, and eventually went together to the Oceanside Hotel (not on the ocean, but who knew from the phone book?). And things happened that night which troubled me decades later as I sat at the Landon dinner table with Bella, Nelson, Jenny, and (the ever vigilant) Taz.

Two specific images rose up to unsettle me: a brown retriever catching a frisbee on the beach and "joint coed naked showering." Like the toothache that seemed worse when I thought about it, these pictures grew sharper as I contemplated them.

The dog's mindless pleasure irritated me on the day I watched the surf with Cindy. He belonged to a young couple (why wasn't *that* guy in Vietnam?) on holiday who'd set out a picnic under a multicolored beach umbrella. The young woman (his girlfriend or wife?) leaned back in one of those short-legged lawn chairs, a sun hat shading her face, and watched man and dog.

The master had perfected a toss into the sea breeze, which the retriever read remarkably well. He watched the frisbee's flight out and up, its turn back from the wind, its descent toward the sand. It never landed, however, as Frisbee (Cindy named the dog later that night) leapt and caught it every time.

"Ah, to have a dog's life," I proclaimed to Cindy and to the world in general, envious of this canine's freedom and his pleasure. Nothing threatened to put a stop to the dog Frisbee's beach-bum existence, an animal who would never be drafted.

"You have that life for, what is it, two more days?"

"Just one. Hey, let's have a drink."

I had beer in a cooler and had not waited for the sun to reach the yardarm, whatever that actually meant. There was something else in the suitcase back in my hotel room--a modest stash of marijuana. (And now you know that the word "joint" in "joint coed naked showering" was not redundant.) It was assumed that even friendly girls in Australia would need some relaxing to do all the things GI's wanted to do in their hotel rooms. And I was following the formula prescribed by lucky Peter Ward all the way. I guess. I think. I assume.

You see, there's a giant blank at the end of my memory of this night with Cindy of

Sydney, most accommodating young person. I remember distinctly doing all the things that precede "joint coed naked showering." There's even a sharp picture of Cindy wearing the tropical shirt I had bought on the beach for her . . . and nothing else.

I recall waking up with a pleasant soreness in all the parts that might have had major roles in soap play. Cindy, who surely knew what had happened in the wee hours, was gone. But she'd told me she had to be home before her parents woke the next day.

Looking across the dinner table at Bella years later, I wondered if there were any blanks in her memory of that time I was (perhaps) being faithful to the nation and (probably) being unfaithful to her. Why was I suddenly convinced there were?

VI.

At noon the next day I glared at my mountain and fretted.

Technically it wasn't (and still isn't) a mountain, especially if you're thinking of the Rockies or the Alps as your models. Missouri's high rock formations are generally the result of erosion occurring over eons. Above lower areas washed away by ancient waters, a once upland country remains in stubborn high ridges and occasional individual rock prominences.

A recalcitrant high mass is what I've got here in the Pacific area, where the Banisters' farm lies and where all the preliminary surveys have shown me I need to put this new road.

There are other kinds of Missouri "mountains," especially south and a bit west of St. Louis near Ironton, where once-molten igneous rocks have been pushed up to create the state's highest ranges. And there are also a lot of east-west ridges shoved along by glaciers heading south in long ago Ice Ages.

Still, if you're building a road in my part of the country and you come up to any of these giant rock masses, it might as well be

49

called a mountain, and it's in the way. Ninety-nine times out of a hundred, the department's budget restraints and environmental concerns say you're not going to move it, go through it, or climb over it. You're going to go around it, even if that means taking out the Banisters' house and barn.

I realize I'm a bit odd in not liking mountains, one of the Show Me State's often touted features. But I insist upon this professional basis for my position: mountains too often block the path of good roads. Generally, I can deal with engineering challenges they present. It's the myriad political objections to taking any route around a big hill that have come to irritate me.

People who wax poetic about "lofty peaks" and "inspiring vistas" are often thinking of scenic parks, places crafted by engineers like me to soften and civilize a harsh environment. Travel agents and wilderness guides close their eyes to how much dynamite is used to create trails and how much gasoline must be burned by earth-moving and tree-cutting equipment to tailor friendly landscapes. I'm a lot less romantic about Mother Nature.

I have sometimes contemplated requesting a transfer to another region, but the rest of the family would surely object. And I recognize that it's best for our children to stay in one high school until graduation. Plus, Bella's new position at Western University is something she's waited a long time for.

Precious few mountains stand in the way of building roads in the northern third of the state. In the flat prairie section of Missouri, you do have to bridge broad, shallow rivers spreading out across the flatlands, and that, also, involves negotiating with residents. But there is no giant rock lump blocking your path, and I'm drawn to such a situation. Too, there has been population loss rather than gain in these agricultural counties for a number of decades, so the highway department mostly has maintenance work to do there, not new construction.

Now, growth did come for our southern areas in the form of middle-aged hippies from the cities dropping out of the rat race and buying goat farms during the Vietnam era. But they didn't want superhighways connecting them to big cities. And most couldn't, in the end, adapt to summers of chiggers, high humidity, and lush poison ivy or to winters of early ice storms and, later, subzero cold spells.

So, my specialty has dictated that I continue to work boxed within the I-70 corridor, that main highway linking St. Louis and Kansas City. And I continue to resent real mountains.

Following the old adage that things skip generations, my son Nelson loves mountains, or says he does. At sixteen, he's the typically unbearable teenage male. So, anything his father likes (a routine, for instance), he despises; and anything Dad hates (say, mountains), he champions.

Whenever we go back to Virginia to visit Bella's family, we cross the Appalachians. And the last couple of times, Nelson has argued for an extra day so we can see more of that old range.

"I'll probably live in West Virginia some day," he announced on the trip we'd taken in August. We were on the turnpike climbing past Huntington. "What colleges are here?"

A junior, he's begun to think vaguely about where he wants to go to school. (The last thing he'll study, of course, is engineering.)

"I don't know about anything except the state university. Where is that, Bel, Charleston?"

"Morgantown," she offers quietly. She doesn't want to get between the two of us, who right now will find a way to argue about any topic. Jenny, three years younger than her brother, sees father-son arguments as a permanent feature of family life.

"You can't go to college until you take the S.A.T.'s," I remind him, not for the first time. I've urged him to try them at least once early, just to see how he'll do. And it's good preparation for the one that will count next fall. Despite his surly attitude around home, Nelson gets good grades and is, teachers and classmates tell us, well liked.

"Maybe I'll skip college. Preston and I want to play music."

Preston is a ne'er-do-well who works--if you can call it that--at the Disc Trick, Nelson's favorite music store. He managed somehow to graduate from high school last spring but says he wants to take their group on the road when Nelson, the youngest, graduates. Preston is their lead guitar; Dan of the always ripped jeans plays bass; deliberately bald Suzanne is the drummer. I can't stand any of them, many times not even Nelson, despite his considerable vocal ability.

Sweet, patient, long suffering Bella tries to calm the waters. "Plenty of time to figure out what you want to do."

"You've got to register with Selective Service pretty soon, you know. There's always a military career."

This is baiting, I know. Nelson has said if he's ever drafted, he'll go to Canada or Sweden. He doesn't understand how that option may not be available for all wars. Sometimes there are no convenient detours around life's big challenges.

Nelson's path into the future remains a concern as he continues school, but the interstate also has to find its way. And my granite mass is too large to bypass to the north. Beyond the Banisters' to the south is the Meramec River basin--expensive, narrow, and tricky to build on. I find myself blocked mentally on this dilemma.

I know I'm blocked with Nelson also, unable to control an anger I don't understand myself. Bella has suggested, gently, that I'm trying to relive my life through my son. But I don't think that's so. Or at least it's not a complete explanation of why I sometimes get so furious with him.

I've been pretty good with how he dresses, the changing hair styles (from conventional to trendy to what I think of as Medusa's untamed snakes). But at least I keep my comments to myself. Well, I unload on Bella from time to time. She's not that happy with her son's current look either, but insists that such rebellion is healthy and probably necessary.

"I hate the hippie look," I complain at one point, again around this same time of the two Phyllises' visit, the Coral Court redux, the lingering toothache. "Remember all those dropout, anti-war protesters?"

"But Mark, you were not all that keen on the war, too."

We're in our bedroom, as I remember, on a regular school night, when I'm wondering if Nelson is doing his homework. Jenny, who would do any if she had some, is in bed reading. I wish she'd take up a serious author (what did we read, *Silas Marner*?), but she's addicted to cheap novels of a girl's first love. Kid stuff.

"Sure, I thought we got in a mess over there, but you didn't see me setting fire to buildings on the campus at Mizzou. Nelson looks like one of those guys I saw in the papers cheering from the sidewalk. Or the one with the torch."

Bella takes a long, puzzled look at me.

"Do you want to talk about it, that time for you?"

"What? Me? No. I'm talking about Nelson here, your son."

I hate it when she starts to psychoanalyze me. She's good for her students, who are going through the difficulties of college-- being away from home, terrible roommates, hard courses. But I pride myself on mental stability. The last thing I need is to lie on a couch and lament my youth, especially to my wife.

Bella gives me another look, another pause. "Your son is just fine," she announces with conviction and turns away.

"Oh, you're such a Pollyanna," I counter, probably just wanting to have the last word in the argument. "If you knew what boys that age are into, you'd be plenty worried."

I know my response sounds hollow, especially to Bella, who counsels teens and young adults professionally. But somehow I need to keep the focus on Nelson. I don't want it on me.

VII.

That weekend I went with Bella to her office at Western University. I didn't promise to eliminate all her worries about the new computerized record keeping, but I was pretty sure I could help her understand how the system should work.

She was facing the same thing a lot of professionals do these days, learning intricate new technologies in which they were not trained. Some of my older colleagues, even though they studied math in college, were reluctant at first to use computers to solve basic problems of, say, soil compressibility or to produce sophisticated programs of traffic flow. They wanted to use the old tools like calculus they had learned as undergraduates.

It may be that, in this case at least, my experience in Vietnam prepared me to meet the unexpected. It's certainly true that what I did there is not what I had anticipated doing.

With my civil engineering degree in hand and later training as a combat engineer at some place like Fort Leonard Wood, I imagined myself in the idealized scenario-- building a modern Vietnam. Other Cold War Americans, I'm sure, believed a similar economic or political story line would guide our efforts to save this distant country from the disaster of Communism.

There was already, we were told, a more democratic government in place after years of corrupt, aristocratic rule. With American advisors and experts at work, the Vietnamese were shaking off French colonial history to become a modern state with vital commercial interests. There was oil, it was even said, in the South China Sea that would be a long-term source of wealth.

I foresaw our superior armed forces first establishing central bases in cities like Saigon, Pleiku, Hue. Then, with the support of the ARVN (Army of the Republic of Vietnam), they would fan out from centers, pacifying smaller cities and towns, villages and hamlets. Finally, even the mountain and jungle countryside would be rid of the dreaded Viet Cong (the VC, Victor Charles, Charlie) and safe from invasion by troops from the North.

This is where I saw myself coming in. Once security had been established throughout an area, engineers would follow the combat troops to repair roads, build bridges, improve buildings. Initially, the goal would be to keep our troops supplied and supported. But then, civilian water supplies would be enhanced, electricity made universally available, modern equipment and methods introduced to Vietnamese agriculture and industry.

Ta-da! A whole new country in the image of the good old U. S. of A. The reality was a bit different, of course, as we all learned at such a cost. We got lost in a vast labyrinth.

Getting out of the car at Western to examine Bella's new computer system, I remembered one phase of Basic Training that should have been a clue to how poorly I had imagined my future military life. In Little Vietnam, I got shot.

At week seven (of the eight-week course) recruits in small groups undertook mock patrols in a simulated rubber plantation, Little Vietnam. It was preparation for the duty most of us could expect to have. We joked about its resembling a Disneyland set, but, as always, there was anxiety beneath the humor. We knew a genuine version of this landscape did exist.

To make the scene realistic, the Army had manufactured indigenous plants out of wood, metal, and plastic, creating a dense jungle environment. Recorded Asian animal calls and bird sounds were played from speakers

59

hidden under fake rocks as a small artificial river wound through the thick underbrush.

Since I did this training in the heat of the summer, the course's artificial flora bathed in Fort Wood's Ozark humidity was realistically tropical. With heavy special equipment and combat fatigues we were sweating like real soldiers as our squad of ten--most still teenagers--advanced single-file down the supposed jungle path.

Camouflaged recruits from another company, in their final week of training, were stationed along our route. Crouching behind rocks and lying under bushes, their job was to ambush us, troops who were only days behind them in military indoctrination.

Their weapons were just BB guns, but they also used tape-recorded sounds of automatic weapons' fire whenever they rose up from hiding to spray us with BB's. The toy guns had curved magazine clips, the recognizable feature of the enemy's standard equipment, Russian-made AK-47's. Scary enough, I found.

We wore special headgear with Plexiglas masks to protect the eyes. Long sleeves and bloused trousers gave the ambushers almost no way to do physical harm to their victims, or so the drill sergeants told us. The point, of course, was to surprise us, to scare us, to instill in us one more time the need to follow the orders of the seasoned combat veterans who would later guide us in actual combat. I learned the hard way (when I got peppered) that I wasn't yet ready for war. Recalling embarrassment on that day, I returned my attention to Bella's campus.

While there were no classes on Saturday, Western's beautifully landscaped grounds were not vacant. Walking from our car, Bella and I saw students moving along sidewalks, and we were greeted by an aide at the reception desk of Bel's attractive brick building. There was always a counselor like Bel on call for emergencies.

And, of course, there are "regular emergencies," if that makes sense. A coed dumped by her fiancé needs to talk; a boy hearing that his parents are divorcing has no one else to turn to; a friend panics when she is unable to wake her roommate who was out partying. And Counseling Services answers the call.

"You don't have to see students today, too, do you?" I asked Bella after she greeted the young woman at the desk and I followed her down the hall to her office. I've tried not to resent those weekends and nights she has to race from home to campus, but it does put a strain on the rest of the family.

"No, James is on call. We won't be interrupted."

Western has only recently changed its status from college to university. Originally a small church-related institution for women, it began admitting men in the 1960s and has grown steadily to more than 4,000 undergraduates. There's a genuine need for a larger Counseling Service and more staff. That--and the fact that our children are both well along in school now--is why Bella has moved from part- to full-time. But when she didn't give up any of her volunteer activities (she's a local president of Mothers Against Drunk Driving, for instance), I worried.

From her office window I see students on their way somewhere--to the library? Dining hall? Parties? The way one of the young women walks along and her general appearance make me think of Debbie McDonald's, and I feel a twinge of guilt. Does she go here? What if I ran into her? Would Bella find out?

Then I remember that I've done nothing improper with Debbie. I just inserted her into a fantasy. No one knows I imagined what it would be like to make love to her. I certainly didn't cheat on Bella with one of her students. Still, a guilty feeling took me back to Little Vietnam and my experience of mock combat.

As our patrol moved through Little Vietnam's training course, I was at the rear of the squad. Pretend Viet Cong, who had black conical hats above their protective face masks, popped up from cover and fired BBs at us. As soon as we spotted "the enemy," we returned fire.

I surprised myself by picking off several ambushers fairly quickly. But then, I realized this happened for the same reason I did better than average in marksman training: I'm not a particularly good shot, but I do have good vision.

Unlike my grandfather, who served in the Swedish Army and was a crack rifleman, I was only a little above average in shooting at stationary targets. But at the final qualifying event, the targets, rough human outlines, pop up at different points down range. Since I saw them quickly and clearly, I knocked more down than most of my fellow recruits, even those who were better shots.

The same ability was coming into play in Little Vietnam. I picked up on the movement of leaf or limb as the fake VC was preparing to rise. And I beat several to the draw, so to speak.

The second time this happened, the weathered, small drill sergeant behind me was impressed and said, "Good shot, Troop." While my consistent policy in Basic was to try to be invisible, to blend in as just any recruit, I'll admit to liking this praise.

After I picked off one more enemy, the drill sergeant said, "OK, Slick. You take point the rest of the way."

Scanning left and right for more attackers, I led the others cautiously. But I saw the last set of ambushers too late, and I suspect the drill sergeant had anticipated my predicament.

The other enemy had been solitary snipers, but now half a dozen VC rose up ahead of me, and more were on both sides. We were in the middle of a (BB) fire fight. The enemy knew what to aim for: my hands (we had no gloves), and my crotch.

VIII.

Western, like many other organizations, was trying to decide at this point whether to go with bigger mainframes or the desktop personal computer. Bella, being new to a permanent position, could only adapt to the arrangement others had established.

The idea that a single miniaturized unit would replace the giant construction--once mainly wires and vacuum tubes, the whole so big it needed its own room and cooling system--seemed farfetched to most administrators in the field of education. So, their idea was to buy more terminals for individual offices, which would be connected to the institution's central computer.

Now, I don't want to pretend I knew at that time where the high tech revolution would lead (which was to the PC). But I know I didn't like this reliance on a single machine, on one system.

Those who wanted the larger, more powerful mainframe saw it as a common resource for the whole organization. But, worried that the shared tool would fail or that its configuration would be biased in some manner, I tended to view the mainframe as a giant labyrinth into which projects disappear. And my work at least, in such scenarios, would never be recovered.

I'd taken this stand at the department, but I couldn't promise that individual units would have the capacity to meet the demands of individual workers or that their combined strength would answer collective needs. Other engineers elsewhere, of course, later made my instinct appear like foresight. Technology was miniaturizing faster than only a handful of industry people anticipated. And my fear of the colossal roadblock for dozens of employees was averted by the microchip.

Bella's school was still committed to the mainframe approach, so what Bella was concerned with was logging onto the system and learning how to enter, manipulate, and retrieve information. As a new assistant director, she wanted to present data that would show increasing need for Counseling Services. She was, in fact, wisely ensuring her own professional future.

"Okay, I need whatever passwords they've given you. And tell me what you know about the filing system." I sat at the terminal stand, which had a pullout keyboard and small writing surface.

Bella was at her big desk, gazing at half a dozen stacks of manilla folders, which made an irregular row on the back edge. If things worked the way she wanted with the computer, all that could disappear or at least go into storage elsewhere.

"It's there beside the keyboard. The handout gives me everything I'm supposed to follow."

"Ah, packed with the latest jargon." As I scanned the several pages of instructions, I explained: "Computers, big as they are, are really just a bunch of wires, each conducting current or not conducting current, live or dead."

"Oh?"

"That's right. Each wire is a switch, see: on or off, one or zero numerically. So, using a binary system, you can represent all numbers. In the base two number system, zero is 'off off,' one is 'on off,' two is 'off on.'"

"I see. I remember something about that from way back when. We're just so used to using the base ten."

I had logged on at this point, but wasn't sure what I was seeing on the screen. Giving this lecture on how computers work had distracted me. And still I went on.

"If you want to do complex calculations, the computer, with its binary number system, can do it electronically. You just enter the numbers, your primary data. There are built-in switches, or gates, programmed to perform basic functions--add, subtract, multiply, etc. So you turn the thing on, electricity travels down all the 'on' pathways, and an answer is presented more or less instantly. Or at least faster than any human could calculate on his own."

Bella had opened one of her files and was thumbing through its contents. "Remember that project I did in my first year of graduate school? I think I wrote you about it. You were in Vietnam."

"Maybe. Did it involve a questionnaire? You know, I'd like to be the guy who figured this out. He should be rich already!"

"The inventor of the computer? Yes. In my graduate school project, I had to use cards with holes at the top to represent data: an open hole was 'yes'; a closed hole was 'no.'"

"Oh, yeah. You run a rod or a needle through the stack of cards, hold the rod up and shake it. All those open-holed cards, the yes's, fall out; the no's stay on the rod. You've found everyone who agreed that, say, the war in Vietnam was unjust."

Not long after that, we went from pulling or dropping cards with holes punched in them to entering data on a card we fed into the computer. Each card was keyed by punch holes to convey data. No more clumsy cards and rods.

I thought suddenly of all the cards it would take to fully represent opinions about that war, Vietnam. What would be the right questions to avoid simplistic answers? How could we separate all the feelings of jingoism, xenophobia, patriotism from altruism, cowardliness, idealism? It would take a building full of cards, a building as big as the Pentagon.

"So I was working with a primitive computer," Bella observed. She had stopped reviewing the files on her deck. And I had stopped studying the terminal screen. "The holes in my cards were like those switches or gates you were talking about--open or closed, on or off, zero or one."

"Okay." I wondered where she was going with this. I was hung up in my contemplation of different mountains of data--about students' psychological states, about traffic flow, about soldiers' destinies, about the shape of history.

"And, of course, the computer is really a woman's invention."

"What?"

"Well, you said a moment ago that some 'guy' should be mighty rich by now, the 'man' who invented the computer."

"That's true. He must be."

"But this sorting system you're talking about is really another version of a loom, for weaving. And that's always been a woman's tool, woman's work. Here, let me draw you a picture."

She pulled a yellow tablet from her desk drawer and rolled over to the computer desk in her office chair. I let her put the pad on top of the computer handout.

"A woman who wants to make cloth--for her family's clothes--and who has a loom, starts by warping the loom. That is, she winds individual threads around the warp beam, a cylinder at the back of the loom."

"Okay."

"Each warp thread is pulled through a heddle in a vertical frame, which is called a harness. There are two or more harnesses. Then, however many threads wide the cloth will be, that many threads are pulled across the loom frame. They can be separated--half alternately pulled forward or pushed back-- by foot peddles connected to the harnesses."

"And different threads are passed through the other way?"

"Yes, contained in a bobbin, which rests in a shuttle. The weaver throws the shuttle through the warp threads, pulling the woof thread behind it through the shed--that's the space between forward and backward threads. Then, a new woof row is pushed down on the warp threads by the beater, which is part of the harness."

I studied the loom she had sketched on the yellow pad and was able to grasp the basic principle, though not all the details.

"The new cloth is wound around the apron beam, here," Bella concluded. "But my point is this separating of threads, those pulled one way by the harness and those pushed back. They're on or off, open or closed, one or zero, just like a computer."

"Oh, I don't think those two things are connected," I said. (Some months later, though, I learned about a French inventor who used punched cards to guide the threads in an early power loom.) "You're just seeing similarity. The computer's a much more sophisticated piece of machinery."

"Well, maybe so." Bella looked at me closely. "But we sometimes see the similarity first and later find there's a more direct cause-and-effect relationship. For instance, the most unusual piece of woven cloth I've worn lately is connected to some important things in our life--your old Army uniform."

"Now, that was interesting. It connected us."

"Yes, it did. It gave us energy, a jolt of electricity." She picked up her yellow pad and went back to her desk. "You know, you never asked me why I wore it."

I hesitated. "Well, that was an idea I had, wasn't it? Doing something different, at the Coral Court, to put the zing back in . . . in our sex life?"

"Mark," Bella said. "One of these days, we really need to talk."

IX.

Maybe we did need to talk, but I wasn't ready on that particular day. Picking up the computer handout and pointing to the screen, I tried to return her attention to the computer and access to mainframe programs.

"You're set here," I said, gesturing to the terminal. "For once, someone has written out instructions that make sense." I suspect Bella, my wife/analyst, knew I was deliberately slipping out of a counseling session.

I concluded she hadn't needed my help in her work either, as everything in this system was pretty straightforward. Together, we sent a short sample file to storage and retrieved it. We couldn't test most of the operations, though, as the university processed its own data over the weekends and took priority over the projects of individuals or small offices.

"Let's go home," I proposed shortly. And she accepted without my having to bring up the fact that my tooth was bothering me again. (Bella would always permit health matters to override other concerns.) She returned papers to folders, folders to stacks, stacks to desktop.

Watching Bella work efficiently, I thought about my own problems and wished they would disappear so easily as this one had for her. More and more I felt vague impasses rising up before me. Even something about her explanation of looms and weaving troubled me, but I couldn't pinpoint it at first. I don't think it had to do with Jenny, but perhaps it did.

Jenny was our athletic child. It's true that Nelson was a better than average baseball player. He had even made JV his first year of high school and won a spot on varsity the next year. But after playing only a handful of innings all season, he'd turned his attention to music, to Preston and "Bulk Order" (that was their band's typically ironic name).

Jenny, on the other hand, was simply dazzling at soccer, so quick and coordinated that a college scout had already come to one of her league games. The high school coach had told us that not only would she start in the spring, but the offense would be geared to her speed and agility. I had a star blossoming just as women's sports were finally being taken seriously!

Or, I thought I had a star. Jenny had lately been talking about not going out for the team and taking up other activities--like embroidery, of all things. I didn't want her trapped in the drawing room, as girls had been in my youth, but out in the action. Oddly, Bella had encouraged her.

"You don't understand adolescence much, do you?" she'd said. She was mostly joking, but I realized that this was a topic she'd studied in far more depth than I had. Again, our exchange was an after dinner conversation over coffee, both kids having gone off to their rooms.

"What's to understand? They don't know what they want. That's where parents come in. We tell them what to do. And I say, go with your strengths. She's an exceptional athlete, and you know it."

"Remember when you worked at that tire shop, years ago? You were in high school, I think."

"Martin's? Of course. What a boring job that was! Same thing day after day after day"

"You've told me. You had to go through books that had not been sold and sort them or something?"

Martin's main business had been retailing tires, new and recapped, for that growing fleet of American vehicles traveling over an expanding network of continent-crossing highways. Route 66 and its traffic were at their peak, before the rise of interstates reduced America's Main Street to access lanes, local avenues, abandoned roadbeds.

"Right. I was an 'inventory specialist'," I chuckled. Big Joe Martin also distributed paperback books throughout Fairfield and Phipps County. Whatever copies didn't sell came back to the tire shop, where I had to classify them as ready to be shipped off for pulp or slated for return and credit from the publisher. Since we had titles from many publishers, consulting a giant master inventory took time--and more patience than an early adolescent generally possesses.

"You hated it. Or at least you thought you hated it. Those long hours. What was it, an eight-to-five Saturday when you were in school, working all by yourself in a windowless room at the back of the shop?"

That was it exactly. Nothing to do for four hours at a time (before lunch or the end of the day) except open box after box of books on a worktable, mechanically sort them into general categories by distributor, then check one title at a time to determine its destiny-- continued life or destruction.

Of course, I did find a few ways to amuse myself, primarily setting aside the occasional racy title that passed through my hands for recreational reading. I skimmed the imitations of *Peyton Place* for steamy make-out scenes (steamy for the 1950s, of course) and cheap copies of *The Naked and the Dead* for models of courage in war. And one time I even witnessed one of Martin's mechanics servicing his girlfriend in a dark corner of the building.

I was able to spice up the day somewhat, but to Bella I insisted, "Those books made a sizable hill in one corner of the workroom. The drivers at Martin's would stack the boxes, but not neatly. They just heaved them in there haphazard."

"You and a heap of books, poor boy!" She patted my hand.

"That kind of work reminds me of why I've always wanted to be an engineer--to build things, things that work, roads and bridges and interchanges." I wasn't willing to take this topic lightly. "So much of what people do in the world is pile up messes. The tires out back of Martin's, a whole mountain range of them with peaks and valleys. It never got smaller that I can remember."

"Yes, but you made your pile of books smaller, didn't you? What you did wasn't challenging, but it allowed you to take action. You didn't realize that the repeated mindless chores gave you time for reflection, time for adjusting to new demands."

"Next you're going to tell me I liked what I did in the Army. As I've always told you, combat engineering is to engineering as military music is to music."

"But why do you think you like to tell that story about the tire shop, anyway, your book inventorying days?"

"That's just one of those generation things. You know, 'In our day, we walked barefoot to school in the snow, uphill each way.' I think kids today have it much too easy, and it's good to explain that it's not always been that way. Jenny will be better off if she stays in soccer, rises to the challenge."

"You're probably right. But she also needs time to be by herself, too, to do some mindless things."

"I find it odd that you, a modern working woman, seem to be training her for an old-fashioned role."

"Adolescents need to be off by themselves for long periods to figure out who they are, what they really want to do. And repeated actions can use up some of the energy being generated by raging hormones. It's not what she does, but the act of doing."

This made no sense to me. I couldn't believe the grinding operation of unpacking and sorting books had ever been relaxing. I just remember wanting to get out of there. And it was the same in the Army.

Well, it was generally the same.

I do remember times in the rear when you wanted each day to be like the last, no matter how uneventful. You wanted the long hours of post guard duty to drag on slowly, so long as nothing happened. Whatever project your engineering company had taken on in the field, each day's routine effort was the perfect model for the next day if there had been no sign of the enemy. "Beware the dog of war," we said, and filled our time with daydreams.

Everyone counted the dull days we had to survive, of course, beginning our year's tour with the comment that all we had left was "364 days and a wake-up." And the elaborate greeting of the grunts, who saw the real combat for long stretches, was a superstitious ritual, linking this moment to a future.

The black man's "dap" involved grabbing, knocking, sliding fists and fingers in an intricate 60-second handshake. It enacted a belief in the soldiers' connection, in their camaraderie, and in life's linkage over time.

When those of us who had better duty saw two weary soldiers going through the handshake routine, we were awed at their courage and embarrassed by a relative safety few would ever consider giving up, even though we had our casualties, too. Ah, Warren Stevens, you are not here today, are you? Bright, kind youth from New Jersey, you did not choose dull routine like the rest of us. How I wish you had!

X.

On the way home I found that Bella was not giving up on her intention to confront the ghosts of our past. She had just postponed talking about that time, my year as a soldier in Vietnam and her year as the one who waited at home for a soldier's return.

The shadowy denizens of that period were increasingly restless after being initially disturbed by the two Phyllises, Orange Man, Taz the Terrible Terrier. My desire for a night at the Coral Court and the Debbie McDonald's fantasy were, I was beginning to see, signs of deeper unease, issues not fully resolved in my life.

Now that I think about it, some of these emerging memories were like that small section of old Route 66 on the Banister farm, reminders of paths taken and roads abandoned. I would learn soon--and keep learning--that I was not the only one in America haunted by his choices.

At first I thought the Banisters were more than a little eccentric in preserving one hundred yards of 25-year-old pavement running behind their house and through a beautifully tended apple orchard. They must have planted these trees themselves years ago.

"We bought this land not long after the war," Ralph said. "No one wanted it after the highway was moved half a mile from here and most of the old road torn up. The highway department did it, I suspect, at the urging of old Will Goodman." He gestured south. "He wanted traffic to come by his gas station, though this was a better way to go. He had good local connections."

"You mean, the old road was more direct and had less incline past that hill?" I gestured toward my nemesis, the Ozark Mountain. We were standing on his front porch during, I think, my second visit, when I claimed to be just checking into how local traffic was integrated with major roads. Sarah was baking in the kitchen and would soon insist I sit down to tea and cookies.

"That's right. Where they rerouted that section, it passed directly in front Goodman's. But the new road ended up being more than a mile longer than the original one. Isn't that crazy? Did I show you the section I preserved?"

And that's when he took me around the house and I saw it for the first time: a stretch of old cement road, worn and cracked in places, but still drivable. The centerline was faded, and the sun had bleached the surface. But Banister must have kept the shoulders mowed and the pavement swept clear of debris, for there were no leaves, twigs, or litter of any kind.

"It's like a picture of America from another day!" I was stunned at his effort to preserve what no one else must have wanted. I also saw how wrong that first project had been from an engineering standpoint. While there was just barely room for the second route advocated by Goodman, it was in the flood plain and couldn't have accommodated the wider roadbed which would clearly be necessary one day.

"We take this walk every morning," continued Ralph. "Sarah, Okie, and me." Okie was their miniature dachshund, a committed (but so far unsuccessful) squirrel chaser. She was inspecting the yard from the porch at that moment.

I said, "A stroll down and back would be good exercise. But that road's more concrete than you need, isn't it? A nice sidewalk would do. And you're not going to meet any neighbors to talk with out here."

"It wouldn't be the same, though." He clucked philosophically, but I wasn't sure why. Thinking only of how to convince him it would be better to live in another place, I hadn't fully grasped the reasons he was holding on to this land and the old road. He was thinking in a frame of reference I didn't recognize at that time, though now it shapes much of what I do every day. And even then, it made me pause.

I recall a similar sense of uncertainty when I first met Warren Stevens. He was an Army correspondent visiting our unit when we were operating out of Fire Base Rebecca. He, too, seemed to be aware of things I hadn't known about.

"Anyone here want to talk to home?" he asked us with a wide grin. He had hitched a ride in with a mail chopper. A portable tape recorder with its built-in microphone sat on the mess tent table where six or seven of us were smoking.

"Talk to home?" said Dick Target. "You can *take* me home."

"Know what you mean. But what I'm doing is interviewing GI's for their hometown radio stations. Just a few questions where you get to say hello to your girlfriend, that everyone's okay here, that you'll be home soon."

"Yeah, right! This war's practically over, Charlie's gone back to the North." Again, we laughed.

"You guys are good here, aren't you?" Warren asked. "You've got armored support. Charlie's not looking for a big fight."

"We don't even notice those rockets into the compound at night. And what mortar rounds?" So far we hadn't had casualties in this operation, and we believed what we were doing would be effective. Today, however, there was too much rain for the big equipment to work.

We were winning the hearts and minds of the Vietnamese people. Or, we believed we were. VC hiding places eliminated, local leaders protected by US-trained soldiers, new services and facilities improving the lives of ordinary citizens. Each of us just had a year to serve, but, if things weren't done at the end of one tour, replacements were ready to finish the job.

"Say, Stevens," Rabbit asked. "Do those tapes really get played back in The World?"

"Sure, the Army's good about that. Everything I do goes through the Hometown News Center in Kansas City, then out to . . . where you from, troop?"

"Des Moines, Iowa," answered Hardball.

"To Des Moines, Iowa, then." He paused. "It gets aired, but sometimes I do wonder how many people are listening."

"What do you mean?"

"Well, . . . " Warren clicked off the machine, leaned back a bit on the bench and scanned the other tables. "I have to be pretty careful about what I ask. And what I leave out of the interview. So what goes on the air is, well, dull."

"There it is."

"My CO says the troops are all supposed to want to be here. They're committed to the job. We don't want the folks back home worrying about us, so I have to edit out any complaints."

"Yeah, makes sense. We're here to win this war. We don't want to give those peaceniks any help. If they'd stop that protesting, this thing'd be over quick enough."

"Let me tell you something, though." Warner checked to see who might be looking. The mess tent was empty except for us enlisted men.

"One time, they sent me down to the evac hospital in Long Binh to talk to guys that had been injured."

We all grew quiet. We didn't want to think too much about those who'd been hit, especially anyone who'd bought it. But there's always a certain fascination with such stories.

"Of course, the guys who are hurt bad, they're medevac'ed out of here. To Japan first, where they can treat, um, the bad burns, the . . . well, you know.

We did know. He went on.

"As soon as they can, they get those patients back to the States. So, I'm talking to guys with appendicitis, flesh wounds, small stuff. These GI's will be back with their units in a few days or weeks. So it's not bad."

We nodded. He paused.

"Two things: the first is how many of these guys there are! You sort of lose track of it wherever you get stationed, unless you're humpin'. At the hospital, though, it seems like there are an awful lot more wounded than you think. I'll tell you something else: it's odd that so many of the grunts are black."

No one contradicted him, though I knew many of the whites saw nothing wrong with this last fact of Army life. When he said it, though, he looked right at Target, who was black. Stevens said things others were afraid to.

"Anyway, one white guy I talked to, his leg was suspended in a sling. He heard all my regular questions--'How are you feeling? They treating you well? What would you like to tell the folks back home?' And, of course, I'm ready to cut off the recorder if he starts saying things my CO wouldn't allow. But, after a minute, he asks me himself to 'cut that thing off a minute.'"

Again, there's a pause we don't interrupt.

"'You know what happened to me?' he asks. I say, 'Wounded?' gesturing to his leg. He says, 'No. Not by Charlie.' He waves me closer, says in a low voice. 'I shot myself. I'm not going back out there. You tell anyone you can, it's hell and I got no damn idea what we're doing over here.'"

Volume II. Dirty Earth. Chapter XI.

What was I doing in Vietnam that, at least so far, had prevented the growth of any desire to shoot myself in the foot and get a "ticket back to The World"? Well, I've already explained what, before I left the States, I had *thought* I would be doing: building roads and bridges in a new, democratic, free-market society, a bastion against the spread of Communism in Asia.

Combat engineers do have specifically military functions, however: managing river crossings, clearing mines and booby traps, destroying enemy systems of transportation. And we are even prepared to fight as infantry, if needed.

But I was led to believe (or had convinced myself) that my unit would be involved in other tasks also traditionally undertaken by the Army Corps of Engineers: construction of navigation and flood control works, management and restoration of wetlands, improvement of highways and bridges.

Because there was still fighting in this country, however, military objectives had to be accomplished before civilian projects could go forward. So, my skills and energy were devoted to a set of tasks I'd not anticipated any more than I had foreseen getting peppered in the groin with BB's back at Fort Leonard Wood.

I never told Bella--or anyone else, for that matter--much about my assignments in Southeast Asia. We all got used to disguising, for our friends and family, the dangers and the fears we faced daily. So, I wrote to her and my parents mostly about guys I served with and comic or ironic incidents that asserted a generally safe world, a world from which I would surely return.

After that visit to Bella's office at Western. I began to wonder if, despite my denials, I didn't want to talk about it after all. "Beware the dog of war," I had said, but the beast still seemed to be sneaking out of its den, my subconscious. Warren Stevens' tales of disgruntled grunts (to coin a phrase), beer guzzling with Billy on my first day in-country, Cindy of Sydney--these ghosts were restless.

But "Don't play in the dirt" had been another of our sayings, an engineer's motto. Like the ubiquitous "There it is" and "Don't mean nothin,'" this asserted: something having to do with this war is undeniable and unpleasant. The rule was that you can point to the painfully obvious, but don't think too much about it. Don't play in the dirt. (The troops' most graphic statement of disillusionment was eventually written on many latrine walls: "Pull out, Nixon, like your father should have.")

In later years I let such coded statements slip out of my mouth occasionally, but few people ever asked what they meant. And I assumed others were as embarrassed to hear about Vietnam as I was to talk about it. There were few veterans in my branch of the transportation department, and we must have shared a common desire to forget our wartime experiences.

We learned a few Vietnamese sayings in our twelve months. "Chieu Hoi" we took to mean "Surrender," though that wasn't completely accurate. "Didi" or "Didi mow" was "leave" or "go quickly." That's what was said to discourage the children who crowded around tall Americans in villages and cities. We figured the majority of those kids were pickpockets, or worse.

There were also a number of stock responses or invitations the Vietnamese developed to communicate with U.S. soldiers: "Nevah happen, GI"; "You want girl, GI?"; "Got Salems, GI?" I realize now that they were articulating our desires more than their own nature. Cartons of cigarettes were the shared currency of this war-torn world, sad evidence of the primitive communication we had with people we said we'd come to enlighten.

I think now of the all the words that piled up on both sides of that irregularly shaped table set up in Paris for peace talks. Two peoples with vastly different philosophies and traditions assembled in print their negotiating demands, their actions' justification. Days, weeks, months of statement and counter statement, argument and refutation, offer and refusal were stacked up--precious little of it relevant to the hearts and minds of the living and dying they represented (or misrepresented).

I decided I would look for the occasion to review some of this with Bella. The ghosts were increasingly restless.

Unhappily, my son, the lead singer of Bulk Order, was also restless. He announced that his band had a chance to play at a nightclub in Gaslight Square, and he angrily anticipated our opposition. But he was right: Bella and I immediately agreed that he was too young to be out late in that neighborhood.

"But that's how you get known, Mom," he argued, picking on the parent he thought more vulnerable. "The Barge is full of musicians and agents who work for other clubs."

I tried to remember what I was doing at his age, growing up in a small town a quarter of a century earlier. I knew I was up to some things my parents wouldn't have approved of, like peeking in neighborhood girls' bedroom windows. But that was a far cry from hanging out with older musicians, most of whom, if you read the papers, were longtime drug addicts.

"Gaslight? Isn't that area a bit . . . rundown?" Bella asked, looking at me.

"I haven't been in quite a while, but I think I read that they've had to close down a couple of places.

"Oh, a crowd got out of hand one night," Nelson chimed in. "But the cops caused the trouble anyway. Most of us are just looking for good music."

I decided not to challenge his use of the term "good." Nelson's music was mostly noise to me, though occasionally he did sing a few folk ballads with a surprisingly lyrical touch. Still, I viewed Bulk Order as a phase he would surely leave behind when he went to college.

In my less optimistic visions of his future, where his singing distracted him from education, I hoped he would at least slide from performance into entertainment management or technology. He was the one in the band who handled the electrical equipment. And it was the managers who made the real money.

The local area I saw as promising, if Nelson really wanted to pursue a music career, was the Mississippi riverfront, where the Gateway Arch dominated the skyline. Thousands of out-of-town visitors came every month to take the tram to the top and visit the Museum of Westward Expansion at the Arch's base.

And along the riverfront there was a developing nightlife, even before riverboat gambling came along. Convention hotels always needed quiet jazz combos or club singers who took requests. That would be a much safer, more dependable environment, one where he might make connections with the powers behind the scene.

I'd always felt Missouri could capitalize even more on its place in American history. Too many viewed it as a jumping off spot for travel to more important places. Pony Express riders were, in this view, headed out of town for the wide open West. And Mark Twain was piloting his riverboat away from home and toward the more sophisticated East. In a sudden, wild flight of fancy, I envisioned my son as the successful St. Louis entrepreneur who reshaped Missouri's image.

As something like the head of urban development, he would coordinate entertainment across town. There would be celebrations of pioneers from Daniel Boone to Charles Lindbergh in a group of related museums. Boone led the white man to fertile lands in the center of the state, and the famous aviator flew mail into and out of St. Louis before persuading local citizens to finance his historic flight across the Atlantic in the *Spirit of St. Louis.*

Lewis and Clark initiated their historic mapping of the Louisiana Purchase from a camp near St. Louis, already a central location for the Western fur trade. So, their return to this city would be featured, a destination rather than a point of departure.

Nighttime shows would pick up the theme of Missouri heroes and heroines in musical performances. Art galleries would feature a new generation of Thomas Hart

Bentons depicting the settling of the prairies, the development of America's Heartland.

Nelson's reach would follow the Missouri Missouri toward Kansas City, I imagined, and go both up and down the Mississippi past Hannibal and Cape Girardeau. He would sit atop a multimillion dollar operation, marketing the Show Me State's geographic and philosophical centrality to the nation.

What I said, however, to my young son and would-be rock star was, "You guys have enough trouble getting together to practice. You'll never be organized enough to get gigs."

As you might expect, this effectively ended our little family conversation. I had a feeling, though, that I would hear from Bella later about my attitude toward my son. I wondered if she'd believe me when I said my tooth was acting up again.

This on-again, off-again toothache was leading me to admit it was finally time to take action. Far more than a toothache, of course, was gnawing away at me.

XII.

"So," I asked cheerily. "Success with the computer?"

Bella was chopping vegetables for a soup. Now that she was full-time, she tried to cook only once or twice a week, but she made dishes we could serve a second time as leftovers.

"Everything went fine. It's going to take a while to enter all my data. But I think I'll get some help from student assistants, if we're careful about confidentiality."

"Right." I was musing about my own problems at work, especially a meeting I had scheduled with the Banisters. I would reveal the state's need to take their land. The dentist's appointment, now scheduled, would be easy to face compared to that.

"Look in the refrigerator and see if you can find some carrots; there should be a full bag. Did you know I see employees as well as students?"

"No, I don't guess I did. You mean the grounds people or housekeeping?" I rummaged around in the vegetable bin--

broccoli, beans, celery, and finally carrots. I handed them to Bel.

"Thanks. Well, yes, the staff can ask for counseling. But I'm actually working with two faculty members."

"Hmm."

I was watching her growing mound of ingredients for the soup: onions, potatoes, tomatoes, green things I couldn't identify exactly. She didn't really follow a recipe, but she liked her soup to have lots of variety. Conscious of recent reports saying we should all cut back on red meat to avoid clogging up our arteries, she was probably making this with vegetarian bouillon.

"When you're at an institution for some time," she went on, "you find out, of course, that there are lots of worries beneath the surface. More people have problems than you realize. And now that everyone knows I'm in all day, my schedule is filling up."

"Well, that's good. You believe in what you're doing, and this shows that there's a need."

"I didn't realize how much some professors feel the pressure--you know, publish or perish. Of course, I remember what it was like to be a graduate student. That was hard."

Wiping her hands on her apron, she scraped two more piles of chopped vegetables to the side and contemplated her project. Bella loved to cook, taking time to shop for the right things and trying new dishes. I was too impatient and would have turned to microwave dinners if it had been up to me.

"When I finished college and the Army, I was ready to get some things done. No more studying about it!"

"Yes, I remember."

Once back from Vietnam and released from the service, I conducted two whirlwind campaigns: one to marry Bella; and the other to start work as a highway engineer. After two hard years in the military, I felt I was owed some rewards.

"I didn't need to study you any more," I said, rising from my chair and coming up behind Bella. I put my arms around her waist and nuzzled her neck. "I was ready to apply my skills, as happened at that exotic Route 66 establishment a few weeks back."

She chuckled and reached around to kiss me on the cheek.

"I was done with my Master's and ready to work too, but Nelson came along faster than we expected." I had returned in the summer, we married before Christmas, Bella was expecting by the next summer. She worked less than a year at St. Mary's.

"And I had my first battle with the I-44/I-270 interchange." I'm not sure anyone ever foresaw the growth of traffic at that crossing. We would finish one expansion only to discover that it had already been outgrown. It was as if cars were coming up out of the ground as well as from the city.

I'd never been in charge of planning there, though I sometimes felt I should have been. Living in the western suburbs, I'd felt I had a good sense of how the greater metropolitan St. Louis area was expanding, how the counties to the west were developing as "bedroom communities." The growth was mammoth, creating horrendous traffic backups that paralyzed commutes.

"You know," Bella said more quietly. "You know, I don't think I realized for a long time that my struggles as a graduate student involved you. I told you before, how hard that was."

"But I was 10,000 miles away, causing you no trouble."

"I know that. But I was thinking about you all that time you were gone. You'd half-proposed to me before you left, remember?"

I recalled the scene quite well, the morning after the Coral Court disaster. We were in front of the graduate dorm at St. Louis University, a moment before I would get in my parents' second car and drive back to Fairfield for that farewell. Dad would take me alone to the airport the following day.

In my thinking then, Vietnam was a blank, not a place. I was going to be absent from my real existence for a year, somewhere. When I returned, life would resume right where it had left off. I think I planned in advance a certain amnesia about my tour.

A lot of draftees felt that way. While we endorsed in general the goal of resisting Soviet or Chinese expansion, we didn't consider it the major focus of our lives. Our parents' battle to stop the worldwide spread of Fascism had been different: everyone was in it for the duration, in service or in support back home. But this "conflict" wasn't even officially called a "war," so we each expected just to do our part and then move on.

Many of us didn't travel over there with our unit. We were individual replacements (called "turtles" by those we would relieve because we moved so slowly). So, the sense of a shared mission and a corporate identity was missing. And I, at least, retreated into a shell for the twelve-month tour.

We mostly flew to Vietnam from West Coast bases (I went from Ft. Lewis, Washington) with stops in Alaska, the Philippines, or Guam. The incredible distances we covered and the flying at night made it seem as if we'd slipped into another dimension, a shadow world from which our return was less certain than we pretended.

On the steps to Bella's dorm, I promised to stand before her again and ask officially for her hand in one year's time. I would not be gone on some glorious adventure, I admitted, scaling Mount Everest or rafting with Heyerdahl across the Pacific. I was just biding time, treading water, hibernating until spring.

Bella resumed her story. "I was so alone that year you were gone, with my family back East. Even though I'd been a good undergraduate, I had to work hard at this next level. It was a much larger undertaking than I'd imagined."

"Didn't I write every week?" I felt defensive. She dumped her piles of vegetables into the stew pot. Adding the liquid, she brought the mixture to within an inch of the top. This would make several meals of leftovers. I hoped it wouldn't boil over.

"You did, you did. And that helped, but I didn't really make good friends there. It was all so competitive. I felt like I needed counseling to get my degree in psychology!"

"Your letters were always cheerful. And you got good grades."

"Yeah, I concentrated. But sometimes, I thought of you and what you were doing, if you were okay."

I didn't say anything.

"I wondered if you would change over there, if you would think about me differently. A lot of people said the guys coming back were not the same. We didn't know about post-traumatic stress disorder, but I feared that this old world, the old me, wouldn't be . . . wouldn't be as attractive."

"All that never applied to me. Didn't I come up to see you as soon as I'd been to see my folks?"

"Sure. But I couldn't know all that time you were gone that that's what you'd do. You went to Australia on R & R, remember? You might have found the girls there more to your liking. Maybe you wouldn't want ordinary old Bella from down South."

All along, of course, I feared she wouldn't want ordinary me from the Midwest! She was probably meeting all sorts of interesting guys in graduate school, intellectual types who would match her desire for a career in academia. Rather than advancing in my professional life, I had been stagnating for a year, stranded on the other side of the planet.

Now I know, though, that I wasn't stagnant at all in Vietnam. The experience did change me. I just hadn't begun to see it until recently. The evolution was hidden so deep inside it had taken fifteen years to make its way to the surface. And it was potentially gigantic, a transformation of major proportions.

I had always been so sure I knew who I was, the open book, a guy who liked to build things (a kids' store in my the neighborhood where I grew up) and remake things (the interior of a Buick station wagon my parents had given me to drive to college). But, I had been turned into a destroyer too, I discovered, a man who tore down what others, including Mother Nature, had made.

XIII.

Bad things come in threes, don't they? Train wrecks, storms, errors of judgment. What about memories?

I'd had two: the dog shot dead in the concertina wire, probably by me; and Cindy of Sydney, a woman with whom I presumed I'd been unfaithful to Bella. Was there a third, more painful memory I was keeping buried? A fourth?

I feared there was. Some of it had to do with Warren Stevens, who was, I knew, dead, Kilo India Alpha. That was bad enough. But there were other incidents--he'd been there, too--even harder to confront. I was letting them hide beneath a decade and a half of pleasant memories from my married and family life.

Oh, I don't mean I couldn't have called up this third set of images from memory on the same day Bella was making soup and I was recalling my proposal of marriage to her. But I knew I didn't really want to.

I had long ago convinced myself no good would come from rethinking what had happened near the end of my tour. The events of the past could not be changed, and I had enough problems in the present. I had, in fact, the magic number of three: the Banisters' grip on their land; Jenny's lost motivation for sports; Nelson's dream of music stardom.

I was supposed to be ignoring Jenny's current backsliding. Bella told me this would be resolved more easily by the two women in the household.

"Okay," I agreed. This conversation went on while the soup bubbled at the stove. She accepted, at least for now, my assertion that I did not change in Vietnam, at least in relation to her. She had been, was, and is the girl of my dreams. "But be sure you explain what an uphill battle Jenny will have if she ignores her own talent," I insisted.

"Don't you think she has more than one talent?"

"Yeah, that's true. But she needs to understand the current of history here, the opportunities for female athletes. I don't think everyone realizes how important Title IX is. Women's sports have to be given equal resources now, but there are fewer girls going out for sports."

The image I had in my head was of an old-fashioned pair of scales: two little dishes hanging by chains from the ends of a crossbar balanced at its middle on an upright rod. The dish for men's sports had always been loaded with gold coins. The other, holding perhaps a few pennies, was lifted helplessly in the air. But now, the situation was being equalized.

I thought also of the seesaw in Westlook Park in my old neighborhood of the Circle. Whenever I chose to use my greater weight, poor Marcia Terrell--a girl from my generation--would find herself high in the air, straddling the plank. By bouncing on my seat, I could also spank her bottom with the board at the other end. Now, if she hadn't taken up the monastic life after our childhood, she would have the power to put me in my place.

"You do remember I work at Western?" Bella said. "We have regular meetings about Title IX and updates at least twice a semester. I understand the social and institutional dynamics. But I also want us to be careful of the individual, of Jenny."

"I just love to watch her run and dribble. It's as if the ball is attached to her foot. She's so smooth in her motions, and the defenders seems stuck to the ground. Sometimes, it's as if there is nothing at all in the way between her and a score."

"You're exaggerating, but I know what you mean. It's just that she has to take care of other parts of her growing up, too, parts you don't know about."

I recognized I would have to give up this argument for now. Bella was going to use the gender trump card: men don't understand how women are constituted. Jenny had gotten her period last year, for instance, but still suffered from cramps. I had once foolishly protested when that forced her to miss practice.

Having grown up in a household dominated by men, I had to admit my superficial knowledge of a woman's distinctive nature. I had never been able to take in the fact that Marcia, my childhood girlfriend, had become a nun. No boy I knew would ever take vows of chastity or silence. It's true that I became, after the Army, a churchgoer of sorts. But I couldn't abandon the scientific approach I got from engineering, and I'd never been hit by an undeniable bolt of faith from above.

Still, I recognized that being an Episcopalian put me in a group of believers, past and present. And that provided a valuable, if unfocused, comfort. Giving up everything, though, to pray in seclusion as Marcia had done would never appeal to me.

So I accepted the fact that my daughter, with her mother's help, would find a way through adolescence, a way different from mine--and, I hoped, from Marcia's. I would devote my powers of persuasion to Nelson and to my new friends, the Banisters.

When I drove down their lane later that week, I steeled myself to tell them the awful truth: the interstate had to come right through their house. They would be well compensated; I swore to make a special effort in their case. And, I would promise to go as slowly as possible with the whole project.

But, shoot, they were already ancient! It was time for them to move to a place without stairs, a place that required no upkeep, a place where they'd always have companionship and help at hand. I bet their children would welcome this development.

"You have children?" I asked when we were settled at their kitchen table, a pound cake and a fresh pot of tea in front of us. Out the window I could see that old stretch of road they had preserved. What a senseless effort!

"We have ten grandchildren, and one great grandchild," Sarah said proudly. "Our three have been blessed, as we were. Let me get some pictures."

"Okay, yes, I'd like to see them." As she walked toward the living room, I turned to her husband. "Of course, each generation grows up in a different world, doesn't it. Changes do come."

"You don't need to tell us about the automobile, the jet plane, travel to the moon," said Ralph with a chuckle. "Whoa, someone wants to play!"

He was referring to Okie, the little dachshund who trotted up with a tennis ball in her mouth. She set it at Ralph's feet, then waited expectantly. Ralph reached down, picked the ball up, and bounced it through the hall toward the living room. Okie dashed in energetic pursuit, despite the age revealed in her graying muzzle.

"That dog! She'll chase that ball as long as we throw it."

"As long as *you* throw it, Ralph," corrected Sarah, returning with an armful of photo albums. "I've never approved of her skidding across the hardwood, and that ball leaves marks on the wall once she's gummed it up good."

"I have a feeling you've brought out just *some* of your albums, Sarah," I teased.

"That's right! We've got a cabinet in the dining room stuffed full. Some are from our parents, but most are of us and our children. We've been married nearly fifty years, you know."

Okie returned with her ball and circled Ralph's chair before setting it down in front of him again. She gave it a shove with her long snout. He caught it and sent it flying again.

"She's a female, canine version of Sisyphus," I joked. "She has to push that ball up the mountain, only to have it roll back down again every time."

"Well, we all have our mountains to climb," Ralph said. Older people are often philosophical like this, and I knew better than to take on a subject that could grow to fill the rest of the day. Since my highway couldn't climb the mountain to the north of them, I had to get on with my difficult announcement.

"I'm going to let you look at just a few pictures in these last two albums," Sarah said. "They show our children coming along in the Depression, our grandchildren long after the war."

I saw pictures taken behind the house. Some, featuring grandchildren, showed the piece of highway they had saved.

"I'm glad you have these photos of your land here," I observed, holding one up. "It will help you remember how it was."

"How it was?" Sarah asked. She could hear a different tenor in my voice. I told myself again that this was the time.

"I'm afraid I have some bad news. Even though we've tried to find a way around it, the improvement of Interstate 44 just has to come through here. The state needs your land. I'm sorry. There isn't anywhere else a six-lane highway can go."

"You mean we'll have to leave, lose our farm?" Sarah asked.

"Again, I wish it wasn't so, but you will have to move."

Rather than getting angry, as I had expected, Ralph just gave another of his chuckles. "I don't think it's going to be as easy as you think, young man," he said with the smile of a man who knew something I didn't.

XIV.

What impasse Ralph Banister saw to the interstate expansion project was a mystery to me. And, despite my inquiring look, he didn't give a hint of the clever precaution I later learned he'd already taken to challenge the state's right of eminent domain. This would prove to be a man who saw the future and took steps to shape it according to his own lights.

"Have some of that cake there, Mark, and we'll worry about this another day."

"Oh, well, I can't stay long, but, thanks, yes, I guess I will have a small piece. We can go over the details about the deal a bit later. There's paperwork, of course, and that takes a while. You'll be given time to find, um, to find someplace else."

He gestured to Sarah that there was nothing to worry about, patting air down with his palm. She raised her eyebrows to him in a question, but, when he again waved away her concern, she poured us all more tea.

I assumed this was just an old man in denial. By the next visit or the one after that, he'd have come around to the inevitability of this change. So, an hour later I left my friendly hosts with pleasant words and pleasant feelings.

Getting in my car, however, I recalled the barrier I had not anticipated in the construction my unit expected to pursue in Vietnam. Of course, the entire U.S. military had not at first thought its engineers would be taking things down rather than putting them up. Ironically, it was the giant vehicle I rode over there that blocked me from building new and improved roads and bridges in Southeast Asia.

My unit spent most of its time in the field, attached to infantry attempting to secure specific areas in 45-day operations. We would be ready later, it was assumed, to build airfields, military camps, and other installations.

My unit also stood down at regular intervals, generally for 15-day periods, on a large base in the rear, a base nearly as big as a small town back home. In the field we were at work, on guard duty, or asleep. Back at base we underwent training updates, assisted in equipment repair, and even had time to enjoy some of the leisure of regular REMF's (Rear Echelon Mother------s).

Our role as engineers in the field was determined not so much by American planning as by Viet Cong tactics. They used jungle habitats close to important cities and military targets as staging areas for their guerrilla campaign.

We'd been unable to track down and eliminate these forces, as they simply changed their hideouts whenever we discovered their tunnels and cave complexes. Our command came up with the strategy of destroying bases and infiltration routes by clearing out whole swatches of the jungle itself. The machine that accomplished that task was the mount I road into battle, the Rome Plow.

This was a giant bulldozer with an oversized cutting blade. That tool was wider than the machine itself, more than five feet tall and as heavy as a water buffalo. Originally designed to cut fire breaks in the States, the Rome Plow could take out even the huge trees of the tropical jungle with massive sweeps and twisting, stabbing motions.

Where tanks had once been stopped by thick indigenous forests, an echelon of Rome Plows could turn six acres of jungle into a field of rubble, called "slash," in an hour. Working closely with our cavalry, we could rout the enemy and leave no sanctuary for him to return to, even if we later withdrew to more fortified positions.

When first used, the Rome Plows tended to outrun troops on the ground. But mounted infantry were able to provide close security for the engineers, who were vulnerable to mines and snipers. Until they had worked the machines for a time, operators were also in danger from falling trees. To lessen such casualties, tubular cages were built to protect the drivers.

Of course, I was not happy to be assigned to a Rome Plow, having envisioned myself in a supervisory capacity befitting my college degree. However, rank determines assignment in the Army, and less educated Lt. Walter James told me to mount up my third day in-country. He'd lost the previous driver in an accident.

The most I could do to soothe my injured ego was to think of the dozer as a souped-up '57 Chevy tearing down Route 66. My driving skills were challenged by the jungle terrain, but I learned quickly, perhaps because I'd had some backroad experience in Ozark terrain with the restored 1953 Buick Roadmaster Estate Wagon that took me to college.

Initially, I was also directed by more experienced drivers like Peter Ward and Dick

Target. A lead driver was usually guided by a helicopter observer, and we were all connected via radio.

"Don't play in the dirt, Landon," Ward chuckled whenever I slipped off course in my first week or got bogged down struggling with the controls. Somehow his vehicle always found the easy track. But I got the hang of my oversized mowing machine pretty quickly and soon was considered a reliable driver.

Like nearly everyone in my unit, I didn't question the value of our operation: clear the jungle, expose the enemy, eliminate the enemy. Again, Warren Stevens, the traveling Army correspondent, was the one who drew attention to parts of a larger picture.

"Tell me about what you do here," he asked on one of his visits. He was considering doing a story on our unit.

"'Area cuts.' That's when we just slash through a suspected VC area. Then, we let our snooping equipment watch for troops crossing the open areas."

"I've got photographer buddies who like to go out on night ambushes and try to get pictures. Not for me."

Our unit had plenty of stories about ambushers being ambushed. Before we began clearing the jungle around us, combat engineers working at construction were routinely attacked from nearby jungle.

"Last time I was here, though, you were cutting right alongside the main road."

"Right. That's to prevent close strikes on supply convoys or troops moving to new positions. Well, and to protect us when we repair the roads."

"I see. You knock down everything hundreds of yards deep on both sides of the route, and Charlie can't fire from cover?"

"We'd be losing troops every day if we didn't do that. That's what happened before we went to work with the Rome Plows. We can use defoliants, but they take too much time."

I didn't particularly want to talk about another kind of operation we pursued, supporting combat action. We were often called on to create landing zones and safe zones around villages. That's where we suffered our highest casualties, especially among drivers.

This was another version of "playing in the dirt" we were not fond of. We imagined

118

whatever distant general sent us out on such operations sitting in an air-conditioned concrete office somewhere in Saigon. In pressed khakis, he didn't worry about getting dirty himself. But we called him a dirty son of a bitch often enough.

In all our operations we worried about mines exploding around us, tunnels collapsing beneath us, our own bomb craters appearing suddenly in front of us. But there were also 200-foot tall mahogany trees that wanted to fall on us or poke their branches through our protective cages. At temperatures routinely over 100 degrees in our twelve-hour work days, dust stuck to us and made mud to match the earth we were tilling.

Poisonous snakes, biting insects, and--one of agriculture's great resources--bees were also hazards. Rather than pollenating crops, those winger stingers were often chasing drivers off their machines.

Of course, I didn't want to admit to Stevens--or myself--at this time that I'd begun to understand my Plow as a barrier as much as a vehicle. That is, I rode it every day, and together we did the job of taking down trees, brush, anything in our way. We were, it appeared, going forward.

But my goal, as I understood America's war plan, had been for me to build things, not destroy things. I was supposed to help put in place arteries of commerce, intercity connections, avenues for people to achieve their dreams. Was that happening?

My only course was to accept destruction as a path to construction, to foresee the day when a devastated landscape would be reclaimed by nature and the Vietnamese people. I was preparing the ground for their national highways, their Route 66's.

Looking at the Banisters' little farm out my rearview mirror as I rode down their driveway to the main road, I hoped I was doing the same thing at home--destroying to create. But given the outcome of America's intervention in Southeast Asia, I couldn't really be so sure about the end result, could I?

XV.

"Hmm," said Bill, studying the X-ray. "I'm going to schedule the root canal. There someone on Watson Road I recommend."

I was upright in the chair, as he'd finished his examination. The tooth looked fine, Bill said, but the surrounding gum was slightly swollen.

"You can't do the root canal yourself?" I didn't enjoy going to the dentist, but, having become used to Bill, I wanted him to do whatever was needed.

"Well, I have done them, but endodontists have the equipment, and they specialize. It's not going to be a pleasant process, though it is relatively painless."

"Okay. I'm tired of the nagging pain; it comes and goes."

Bill told the receptionist over the office intercom to see what dates were available. I remembered my last visit here and my stop at McDonald's. If I went to the drive-through today, would I see Debbie, inspiration for a fantasy rendezvous?

"This will take several visits," Bill went on, unclipping the paper bib around my neck and stripping off his latex gloves. "They have to hollow out the root, then put on a temporary crown. Later they fill the tooth, and finally comes the permanent crown."

"Most things don't have instant fixes," I agreed, thinking of the Banisters, my children, even Bella. I knew she had more to say about the time I was overseas, her first year as a graduate student far from home. I supposed I shouldn't really be thinking about Debbie McDonald's.

"Try to tell that to our young people these days," Bill laughed. "Their worldview is defined by the 30-minute situation comedy, with everybody happy before the final commercial."

"I know what you mean. But they are living in a lucky time--prosperity, opportunities in technology, no war unless you count the Cold one."

"And they don't even get drafted any more."

The way he said it made me look closely at Bill. "That happen to you?"

"Sure did. Accepted to dental school one day, shining boots at Ft. Campbell, Kentucky, the next."

"I didn't know that. I was drafted, too. Son of a gun!"

Again I was reminded of leaving Bella behind, first to go to Basic, then to Advanced Individual Training, and finally overseas. The two-year hitch of the draftee was the shortest term of enlistment, but it was a heck of a lot longer than a television show today. And Vietnam became America's longest war.

"You go to 'Nam?" Bill asked.

"Yeah. Came back to work for the highway department. Don't think about it much. Or at least I didn't use to."

"It's the same for me. The other day I heard 'We Gotta Get Out of This Place' on the car radio. Golden Oldies station. I bet all the kids listening think the song is about leaving home, but it took me right back there." He paused. "The Nam."

Bill had perched up on his stool, apparently in no hurry for his next patient.

"The Animals' classic," I agreed. "We sure heard that often enough. Who were you with?"

"I was pretty lucky. Hospital in Cam Ranh Bay. The Army found out I could type and knew something about medicine. So I ended up keeping records for a few hundred thousand personnel."

"I was an engineer. At least they gave me the right MOS, but I did a lot more land clearing than road building. Still, came back with everything I took over there."

"Hmm. Funny we didn't know about each other, that we're both Vietnam vets. We even go to the same church!"

"I put it behind me as soon as I was home. Got married that first year, started a family pretty quickly."

Did Bella put it all behind her, I wondered? Was she concerned about what I'd done over there, even after all these years? Since I didn't talk about it, did she think I was hiding something? Did she worry that I had a potential to go bonkers, driven by flashbacks to sudden violence? I did have unpleasant dreams now and then, but everyone does.

"We could get together some time and talk about how it was, if you like," Bill said. "It's hard to explain to anyone who wasn't there . . . how we all felt."

I left agreeing that we'd go out for a beer one evening soon. We could talk about a time after church this weekend. I would have to remember to go this Sunday, though, as I wasn't terribly regular. I blamed that on Nelson's reluctance to accompany us.

I'd gotten pretty good at blaming Nelson for a lot of things in my life. Whenever I was grumpy or short with Bella or Jenny, Nelson's behavior could be cited. His hair, his "music," his attitude. Even failures in my sex life were his fault.

Driving away from Bill's office, I deliberately avoided the McDonald's. No sense daydreaming about some made-up girl when I had a real live woman at home, a woman who loved me. Maybe I'd swing over to Ted Drewes' Frozen Custard, though, a St. Louis landmark along Route 66, and enjoy one of their desserts.

What had Bella said about the Coral Court, wearing my old uniform? I'd claimed she dressed up to excite me, but she hadn't confirmed that exactly. Maybe there was something going on there I hadn't thought about. I would ask her.

Driving, I recalled that earlier episode.

"I knew women fell for men in uniform," I'd said after my "reenlistment." We were side by side on the bed, gazing toward one of the Coral Court's pyramid-shaped glass block windows. "But now I can see how men are vulnerable to women soldiers."

"When you came to see me, on the way to Ft. Bliss, you wore civilian clothes. Same thing on your leave before you went to Vietnam. I'm not sure I ever actually saw you in uniform."

"I guess I was more comfortable that way. Uniforms are starched, and everything has to be strac."

"'Strac'?"

"Sorry. Military term for perfect, passing inspection. Now that I think about it, I don't know where it comes from."

"A lot of people were opposed to the war by that time. Were you worried about what others would think of you?"

I considered that for a moment. In public places I was conscious that my uniform marked me as a member of the armed forces, as part of what we used to call jokingly "the military-industrial complex." Soldiers were scorned by the radical anti-war types, of course, but I knew I wasn't part of their crowd.

"I don't think I was embarrassed to be in the Army, but it sure wasn't like it had been for the men of World War II."

126

I recalled the famous photograph of a returning sailor bending a woman back for a VE-Day kiss in New York's Times Square before jubilant onlookers. The troopships were welcomed by huge crowds on the piers; parades went down small-town main streets; celebratory picnics and church suppers were everywhere. My return had been utterly without fanfare.

"Things weren't the same for the girls back home, either."

"Oh?"

"Sure. In the Second World War women went to work in factories while the men did the fighting. And they were praised for supporting the war effort."

"Oh, yeah. Wasn't there a poster campaign or something?"

"Rosie the Riveter. The government recruited young women for their strength in a patriotic effort. Rosie was pictured with her sleeves rolled up, flexing her biceps."

"It wasn't like that for you?"

"Not at all. If you had a boy in the service, generally on a college campus, you kept quiet about it. People didn't want to ask, fearful that something bad had happened. And some even thought it was wrong to go. They said

127

you should avoid the draft, go to Canada, become a conscientious objector."

"I couldn't do that."

"I know. But I was sort of in limbo back here. That and how hard graduate school was. At one point I was ready to give it all up and go home to my parents in Virginia."

I'd never known about the depth of her anxiety until then, our second night at the Coral Court. Her letters to me had always been upbeat. It sounded like an exciting time to be in graduate school. Now, approaching Ted Drewes' Frozen Custard, I had a different picture, someone who wanted to get away from something perhaps as much as I wanted to finish my tour and come home.

I pictured Bella sitting in a small dorm room, bare walls and one window, kind of like a prison cell. She was reading a letter I had written (marked "free," the same as Tony Robert's tape). It was all about me and my troubles.

And then I imagined her singing along to The Animals' hit. If it was the last thing she'd ever do, she'd get out of this place.

XVI.

The Ted Drewes "Concrete" (an extra thick milk shake) tasted as great as always (though I had to keep it away from the sore tooth). But, it didn't constitute a remedy for all my worries. I would now, for instance, have to ask Bella more about her past life in order to understand her current state.

I got sidetracked from that intention, though, when I came in on the Landon mother-and-daughter team. It looked as if they had been tied up together with embroidery material.

"What's this?" I asked, waving a hand at the piles of yarn and thread that surrounded them on the den couch. "You look like workers in a textile mill where the machines have gone berserk."

"Oh, Daddy, we're just looking at different things I can do. Embroidery, crewel, samplers." She drank from a can of Coke.

"If Taz gets tangled up in that stuff, you won't be able to do anything!" Our terrible terrier was lying on the rug, nose ominously pointed at the sofa. If the doorbell rang and he followed his usual mad route toward the sound--jumping up on the sofa and sailing over one arm toward the hall--they'd wish they were knitting a single small pot holder.

I sat down in my favorite easy chair, surveying Bella and Jenny and their new possessions. From overhead came a thumping sound--*ba-boom, ba-boom, ba-boom.* Could that be drums?

"Bel?" I asked, pointing toward the ceiling.

"It's some kind of African drum. Nelson says he's going to help out with Bulk Order's percussion."

Oh, this made sense! Deliberately bald Suzanne already had a gigantic set of drums. And it seemed to me that Preston and Dan played guitar and bass mostly by banging on all the strings as hard as they could. (I was surprised they didn't break their instruments at the end of each set!) Now Nelson would be adding to the rolling thunder.

I saw pieces of fabric spread across Bella's lap. Some were large enough to be bedspreads. "Jenny wants to take on something substantial, a big project," she said. "Maybe a quilt or a hanging of some sort."

"Well, okay, but you don't want to get too tied up with this, Jenny. You'll have to fit it in around school and soccer. It's going to be a great year for you in soccer, you know."

"I think I've done enough of the samplers, Mom. Even though they're not all perfect, I do want to start on something that will take time, maybe even the rest of this school year."

"Sure," I interjected. "You don't need to be in a rush to finish. Just work some on it every week or so. It's amazing what you can get done that way."

Okay, I thought, so maybe this is just something to do on an occasional evening, after practice and homework. She'll "knit one pearl two" (if that's the right phrase) for half an hour before sleep. I'd rather she watch game film, but this would be a phase she'd pass through, especially once the season actually began. I couldn't imagine the excitement of big games and road trips not dwarfing this new hobby.

"I think crewel may be what you should try," Bella said, though she had to raise her voice as the hollow sound of Nelson's playing had increased. *Ba-boom, ba-boom, ba-boom!* Even Taz was glancing toward the stairs, perhaps expecting a crash of furniture or boxes tumbling down. "You work with woolen yarn, stitching onto fairly substantial cloth. It's not so fine as other styles."

"Do I make the design?"

"You can, of course, but there are also some traditional patterns that may be easier. There's the country village or Shaker farm scene. I think it would be nice to find a design you might hang in your own room."

Good grief! This led me to imagine Jenny's room remade for a girl from the Victorian era. Could I get away with proposing a canvas of famous sports figures instead?

"Hey, I could do mountains and give it to Dad!"

"No, no! Nelson's the one who loves mountains. They get in the way of roads for me. Now, rolling countryside and a beautiful highway snaking out into the distance--that's fine." Right then I could easily imagine a crewel bedspread muffling Nelson's drumbeat with embroidered mountains.

Perhaps Bella would realize he was disturbing the neighbors and spare me from being the bad parent for once. She could try telling him to practice a little common civility.

The highway in the distance I was picturing for a moment on Jenny's canvas is a favorite image of mine. It goes all the way back to my childhood in the Circle. With neighborhood pals like Billy Rhodes I hiked into the woods on a regular basis. We lived on the western edge of town, so views from hilltops that way were all of distant farm and forest. Jenny could do this scene for me!

If we walked perhaps 45 minutes--past Springers' Pond, the High and Low Trails, the college's demonstration mine--we would reach a spot we called "The Open Place." From the top of that ridge we could see for miles. Below us the Missouri-Pacific Railroad descended from the Fairfield Plateau and wound toward the distant Gasconade River. It was a peaceful scene.

Running parallel to the tracks in those days had been John Steinbeck's Mother Road, the same highway old Mr. Banister had saved a portion of on his property. He planned to continue getting his kicks on Route 66, but I knew better. Ours was a world of interstates and nonstop travel now, not two-lane roads threading between barns and farmhouses before heading right into the hearts of America's small towns.

I remembered those Burma Shave signs, spelling out shaving cream jingles along the highway. Each poem was printed in little phrases on signs set a hundred yards or so apart. You read as you rode. I couldn't remember a specific ditty, but my mind's eye added the little red wooden billboards to my tapestry of the past.

The Burma Shave signs kept on for years, an incredibly successful advertising campaign. I suppose it had to be given up when the speed of travel exceeded the nation's reading skill.

There was a place back in my home town that did something similar, Fanny's Dairy Delite. The store, an ice cream shop like Ted Drewe's Frozen Custard, was along Business Route 66, but they put their signs out on two-lane roads all around the state. There was one I've always remembered, though I don't know why: "If your hopes are tumbling, / and your tummy's grumbling, / come build a cone / of Momma's own / at Fanny's Dairy Delite."

"Hey, Bel, you remember the Burma Shave signs?"

"Of course. 'Don't take that curve / at 60 per; / We can't afford to lose / a customer! / Burma Shave.' There was also one about an unattractive husband that ended, 'Shoot the brute / some Burma Shave.'"

"Very good! How do you remember so many things?"

I didn't mean just highway signs. My wife has an incredible memory, perhaps a photographic one. My recollections must be very selective.

"I don't know, dear. Jenny, take a look at this book of patterns. See if there's one that you'd like to do. I'm going to ask Nelson to tone it down a bit upstairs."

Bless her! She's even taking Taz with her. This is a chance for me to work on Jenny.

"I remember my grandmother doing embroidery," I told her. "In the little house she lived in after my grandfather died. I think lonely old women go in for this sort of thing."

"Um-hmm." She was studying the book Bella had given her, turning the pages slowly.

"And in the old days, of course, women had to sew everyone's clothes. There weren't any factory-made shirts or dresses. Why, sewing and other chores like that took up any leisure time a woman had after cooking and cleaning. They were inside the house all day. Sure is good things have changed for your mom, and you."

"Um-hmm."

"You know, even my mom had to work every day while Grandpa was at the office. She made all the beds, washed the breakfast dishes, did laundry--which she had to hang out on the line, summer and winter. Whew, those were hard days."

"Um-hmm."

I omitted the fact that my mother had worked during the war, not as a riveter like Rosie, but in a clothing factory in New York. Sometimes I forget that phase of her life.

"Once, we had a wringer-washer. Know what they are?"

She glanced up at me, but said nothing.

"There was a tub in which your clothes got clean, but to get them dry enough to hang out, you had to crank them through a wringer. Sort of like two rolling pins, one on top of the other. You feed the clothes through, squeezing the water out."

"I'm going to do the country village, " she said, bouncing up from the sofa. Upstairs, the drums were even louder than before.

XVII.

When Bella came down the stairs, having conferred with Jenny on the landing, I raised my eyebrows about the drumming, which had stopped.

"He says he has to take a break now anyway." She allowed herself a smile and a wink. "His hands hurt."

"I suspect Jenny's hands will hurt too when she gets into her country village wall hanging or whatever."

"You let her alone. This is good for her. And it doesn't mean she won't play soccer in the spring. Now, come help me get dinner ready."

"I'm going to fix myself a scotch. You want anything?"

"No, I have this iced tea." She picked it up from the table at the end of the couch. "You okay with Hamburger Helper? Frozen peas? Brown 'n Serve rolls?"

"Sure." I clinked ice into a glass and gave myself a generous slosh of J & B to take the edge off my worries. "How's work?"

"I sure do stay busy! But I've got a student entering data at the terminal several hours a day. Once we're caught up there, I hope things will go more smoothly. It's a hump to get over."

"I need to get past my current hump, too."

"That old couple? The Banners?"

"The Banisters. Yes, the ones who are going to lose their farm. Gee, I feel like some Depression-era banker, foreclosing on a hardworking family. I could be in *The Grapes of Wrath*."

Bella was browning ground beef in a skillet, studying the instructions on the side of the box. "That's silly. They're in the way of progress, that's all. They're not like the Cherokee, made to march the Trail of Tears from Georgia to Oklahoma." We'd been reminded of that historic injustice on a recent vacation.

I recalled the Vietnamese for whom I had leveled forests. Did they end up with places for their grandchildren to visit? Or had we actually been putting roadblocks in their way? What they wanted, we learned eventually, was the continuation of their own culture, a way of life different enough from our own that we didn't understand it.

I sipped on my drink, watching Bella get out the dishes. This woman was continuing

138

her culture, doing pretty much what her mother and grandmother had done before her. True, it was easier now with cooking shortcuts, microwave ovens, processed foods.

"Those faculty you told me about, they making progress?"

"Well, maybe. It takes time with middle-aged people. The troubles are generally buried pretty deep, and often they get used to coping without confronting their problems."

"Here, I'll set the table. Maybe you come to terms with these things just by getting older. Ralph Banister should have been crushed by the news that the highway's coming through his house, but he hasn't been upset at all. He's completely at ease."

"But it's bothering you?"

"I feel sorry for him. On the other hand, he's at an age that keeping up his place has to be getting hard. It doesn't seem like any of their children live close enough to help."

I thought again of my work in Vietnam. I know we destroyed homes and even had to move some villages with our land clearing. And now we've had to admit that our efforts involved considerable environmental damage to the countryside.

It's odd that I'd never thought about the possibility of my having been affected by Agent Orange, the toxic defoliant we sprayed over thousands of acres in Vietnam. I knew I was in areas where it was used, but I'd had no physical symptoms that might be attributed to exposure.

The people I worked with had put their faith in the Rome Plows, which did more than strip leaves from plants. Sprayed foliage did die, but that took time. We provided instant open areas where all cover was gone.

"Didn't you say you liked the Banisters? They were everyone's grandparents."

"I did say that. Maybe that's it: I'm taking it personally, as if they're my own parents and I'm evicting them. But there are larger forces at work. The county, the state, the nation, really, are the big agencies overwhelming the desires of a single couple."

"Explain that road in their field for me one more time."

"Okay. They have some crazy idea about protecting a relic from the past. That stretch of pavement doesn't serve any purpose. You can't drive anything but a lawn tractor on it."

I sucked on the ice at the bottom of my glass and wondered if I could sneak another drink before we ate. Bella would notice, though, and that might lead to unpleasant discussion later.

I don't think I've ever drunk too much on a regular basis. I've gotten sick, not happy, with too much booze. But if there was ever a time in my life when substance abuse was a danger, this period of early mid-life strain would have been it.

Drinking hadn't answered my worries in Vietnam, though I downed my share of Falstaffs in the E-5 club. Whenever we were in the field, of course, there just wasn't time for much of that. And we were never *not* in the field for very long.

"Of course, I'm from Virginia," Bella reminded me. "So I don't have the same associations with Route 66 that people in this part of the country do. Williamsburg and Appomattox Court House are my symbols of the past, of American history."

"Um-hmm. And people have restored those sites so you can revisit yesterday. We don't do that so much out here."

While I'm pretty sure now I wasn't pickling my brain with drink, I do sometimes wonder if I've occasionally suffered from a chemical imbalance deriving from my war experience. Was there a residual presence in my bloodstream from, say, Agent Orange, that clouded my judgment at the time of the Banister project, Jenny's embroidery phase, the beginning of Nelson's music career, Bella's resurrection of her graduate school life? I certainly blundered along for quite a while without processing all the information I was recording.

Frank Middleton, another of the Rome Plow drivers, sometimes acted as if his brain had been scrambled, but we were pretty sure it was drugs he took deliberately, not dioxin by accident. At least, he was conscientious about driving sober, scheduling his major binges for extended off-duty times.

Middleton was a sad case in other ways, too. A skinny, pimply kid from Oklahoma, he'd been picked on throughout his Army career. And probably before that. In some ways driving a Rome Plow was the great success of his life.

Bella asked, "Didn't you once want to take me to that famous Route 66 hotel in Fairfield, the Banner?"

"Yes, that was a grand establishment. Gone now, though. I had a friend who worked there once. And I did a research project in high school about it."

"You think it's sad that it's gone?"

"Oh, I don't know. We've got the Holiday Inn, the Howard Johnson's, the major chain places."

"Just like all the other little towns in America." She turned the stove off, glanced at the clock. "Get the kids."

I set my empty glass by the sink and went into the hall to call up the stairs. We had a peaceful family dinner with no one attacking contemporary music, the skill of embroidery, the practice of psychology.

After supper, passing the closet at the top of the stairs, I recalled Tony Roberts' tape and his voice from "the world of hurt." He was having no satisfying family dinner now, but he was also free from all troubles. Tony's escape from the worries of a combat zone had been pot.

Marijuana was readily available there, of course. And troops were always supplied with beer, shipped into the country as steadily as munitions. Harder stuff could be purchased, too, if you had the cash and needed the hit. So the ways of escaping reality each night were numerous.

As a hopelessly literal-minded person myself, I accepted at face value the view of my parents' generation: marijuana inevitably leads to harder stuff--heroin addiction. There was a sequence of temptations that escalated in each phase. The habit expanded until, in its final monstrous shape, it crushed the user.

Tony enjoyed the mellow high he got with each joint. And I'm sure he would have enlisted in the next generation's campaign to legalize marijuana if he'd survived and returned to the World. Unfortunately, survival was a hump he didn't get over.

The humps I faced now were, in comparison, little ones, regular challenges of mid-life career and marriage. Why was I so glum about it all? Couldn't I put things in perspective, large versus small in the grand scheme of things? "Get on with your life!" I instructed myself, knowing at the same time that it wasn't nearly as easy as I was hoping.

XVIII.

Several weeks later I told my highway department superior in Jefferson City, Jack Taylor, that I was delayed in securing the right of way for the new section of interstate. This was hardly unusual, and we both assumed the same outcome. So, when he called from the state capitol to say I'd better go out to the Banisters' again for one more talk, I was puzzled. This was only a few days after Bella had asked about the situation.

"Jack, you know he can't prevent our going through there," I explained over the phone. "And you also know it's the only real route we have for a road of that size."

"All I can tell you, Mark, is that I've got a handful of state legislators saying something about the federal government's getting involved."

Among Jack's many responsibilities was helping find the 10 per cent of building costs the state had to raise for interstate projects. The Federal Highway Trust Fund paid the remainder.

"We've had the public hearings, we did the environmental impact study, the plans have been well-circulated. Even those guys at the federal level wouldn't step in now. What's going on?"

"Talk to Banister. Apparently he's been in touch with all sorts of people, and they're at least listening to his argument. So he's probably the one who can lay it out for us. I'll try to calm the waters up here."

As I headed west one more time on I-44 toward Pacific, Missouri, and my pseudo-adopted grandparents, I concluded that all this was just denial on Ralph's part. He was pretending he had options but probably understood how it had to end.

He'd been around quite a few years, so maybe he had some friends with connections. He might inspire a final review. But once all the relevant information was confronted, I was confident the state of Missouri and the United States of America would win the battle with one eccentric old-timer and his wife.

The wind had a definite chill in it as I stepped from my car and walked toward the Banisters' front porch. Though lights were on and the house looked occupied, no one came to the door. I found my likable couple out back. Wrapped in winter coats, they were standing on the edge of their private backyard highway.

"You were in the military, weren't you, son?" asked Ralph before I could even get started with my questions. Sarah nodded her usual friendly hello.

"I did two years with the Army, yes."

"Vietnam, I bet."

"Yes, but . . . did you just figure that based on my age, when I would have served?"

"It's more than that," Sarah commented. "You have that way about you."

"That way? What do you mean?"

But Ralph ignored my question and asked another of his own. "Do you know the role of this road in World War II? That was my son's war. And my nephew's."

Sarah turned away from me and gazed out over the mini-highway to the fields beyond. On our right loomed the Ozark mountain that was dictating my current, unpleasant course of action.

"I know that Fort Leonard Wood, which is on the highway, was built up a lot during the war. Were there other installations along the highway?"

"Oh yes, there were quite a few, not just in Missouri but Texas, New Mexico, all along the way. We weren't really prepared for war, you know, when the Japanese hit us at Pearl Harbor."

"We were hoping to stay out of the conflict," I agreed. "But we had been supplying arms to the Allies."

"That's right. After Pearl Harbor, of course, there was no choice. And Roosevelt inspired everyone to the common effort, men and women alike."

I remembered Bella's talk of Rosie the Riveter. My own dad had served three years in the war, but he didn't talk about it very much. Still, I knew people sacrificed, rationing gasoline and certain foods, doing without new cars as our manufacturing was switched to producing tanks and Jeeps and ordinance, planting victory gardens so more food could go to the troops.

Ralph went on. "So, along this highway we had new bases being built and old ones expanded. Plus, factories were refitted for the development of munitions, and new plants sprang up to increase overall production. There was tremendous growth, without which we would have lost that conflict. The German war machine was the greatest ever created."

"Well, Ralph, we're seeing growth now, too. We can't let the Soviet Union have better weapons than we do. And they're putting all they've got into missiles, bombs, delivery systems."

Obviously, I thought I saw an opening here, a way to turn this unexpected topic toward the necessity for a new, wider, safer interstate highway on the only path available.

"Troops went down this highway headed for the Pacific Theater, for Midway, Guam, and Guadalcanal," Ralph said. "Thousands from every little town in every state across the country. Some traveled on the trains, I know. But they finished paving all sections of the road in about 1938, and this became the trail of destiny."

I could hear a melancholy tone in his voice even as he celebrated the country's commitment in that world war. I appreciated what my father's generation had done, too. But what was wrong with modernizing this road? Surely he couldn't think we would want to send new fighting vehicles, new artillery pieces, new airplane parts across his backyard to confront the Russians?

"But Ralph, we have to move on. We can't preserve the past, this one piece of history."

He turned to me with a sudden, bright smile. "Of course we can, Mark. And that's exactly what's going to happen. Come on in; let's have tea and I'll explain." And he did.

Ralph had petitioned the National Park Service to make this section of old Route 66 a protected historic site. With Sarah's and his children's consent, he was ready to will the entire property to the government, should the Department of the Interior confirm its status as national monument.

While he hadn't gotten an immediate acceptance for his proposal, it had been officially recognized as a concept worthy of consideration. Nothing could be done until the review process was completed. And that would take months, at least.

Banister knew that the official existence of Route 66 was coming to an end, the few remaining active stretches being replaced by interstate. If those famous Route 66 road signs had to come down, he argued, all the more reason to designate one place that preserves its importance and teaches future generations about the road's contribution to America in the twentieth century.

I had to give it to him: he'd thought ahead and taken action. There was, I felt, not the slightest chance anyone would listen to his scheme, but he made it sound good with his zeal.

"We knew about the road during the Depression, though we never joined those heading for California," Sarah explained. "It connected so many travelers who stopped at the small motels, who ate in downtown cafes, who filled up at the local gas stations."

"We've lived close to the highway all our lives," Ralph added. "Our daughter followed it to Tulsa when she got married. She lives there now."

"And, like Ralph said, our son and nephew rode it as soldiers in the war. We have to remember what it's done." I didn't know then that her nephew had been lost at Iwo Jima, and that sad fact added to her insistence that Route 66 itself should never die.

When I opened the car door to leave their farm, a vision of the future rose up before me. Instead of the smooth stretch of road winding across the country I'd pictured in Jenny's crewel hanging, an endless, rising succession of mindless government meetings loomed ahead of me, pitting the National Park Service against the state highway department.

I'd be explaining to committee after committee that we had no alternative.

Someone from the Park Service would talk over and over about preserving the past, keeping a record of history. Both sides would have handouts and slides, testimony and rebuttal, requests for more information and promises to meet again.

And I saw mountains of paperwork growing around me. For each meeting I would prepare papers, and afterwards reports would have to be filed. Emendations would be offered, and different offices would receive copies.

And I'd thought Bella's stack of client files was cumbersome! Would the highway department grant me space on the mainframe for proper documentation of this project, or would I build my own warehouse for the swelling Banister/interstate debate?

I closed the car door, sighed, and started the engine. My tooth was aching again.

XIX.

This troubling visit with the Banisters brought back another Vietnam memory: the mama-sans' legendary chicken dinner, which had also supplied its share of the unexpected.

Each hootch in this base had two mama-sans--Vietnamese women authorized to enter the compound and work for whatever wages they could negotiate with individual GI's. During the times we were standing down, I gave them a carton of Salem cigarettes to wash my clothes, shine my boots, and make up my cot. Ironic, isn't it, that U.S. troops passed Army inspection through the paid labor of our host population!

I think the mama-sans kept enlisted mens' quarters clean sweeping and picking up trash, but the exact details of this business deal are lost to time now. I can't really itemize their duties, and I for sure can't tell you what a carton of Salems turned into on the black market in Vietnamese piasters, military scrip, or U.S. currency (dollars, of course, were strictly illegal in-country).

I do know that we sometimes had extra chores for our faithful (captive?) servants. If we were slow returning to the field--because of the weather or scheduled lulls related to combat conditions--we would sometimes organize primitive unit parties that generated giant messes. The mama-sans worked extra hours to remove piles of our trash.

A party mostly meant excessive beer drinking, though we did sometimes cook steaks over charcoal fires in discarded fifty gallon drums sliced in half. I don't remember how we got charcoal, though I think it was a standard source of cooking heat for the Vietnamese.

While we did consume plenty of food at these feasts, more beer inevitably went into or through GI's. And dogs were also big drinkers on such occasions.

Many units had pet dogs. If I remember correctly, not long before this time we had adopted a medium-sized mongrel we named "Westmoreland" (the general who regularly assured us we would win the war and go home soon)--"West" for short.

Dogs survived on bases by eating scraps we discarded from uninspired mess-tent offerings. The troops also shared their beer with their pets, especially at parties. We covered the bottom of an old tin with two or three ounces and then laughed at the wobbly, unsteady gait of our "general."

Beer purchases were rationed for enlisted men, so getting enough Carling Black Label for a good party took some organization. Each GI was authorized to buy one case a month from the base PX, though you could get as many individual beers at the E-5 club as you were able to pay for each night, so long as you drank them on the premises.

To provide enough beer at the hootch for a party, we had to pool the monthly rations of half a dozen GI's. We'd pack the old refrigerator stuck in a corner of the hootch with maybe 250 cans and promise to make it up later to those who'd used their rations.

On rare occasions, we could talk a low-ranking officer into buying hard liquor for us, which was strictly against regulation. Again, while enlisted men could drink all the bourbon or scotch we wanted in the clubs, we were prohibited from buying our own--military discipline, I'm sure.

I remember coming back from my R & R in Australia and passing by a supply center on Tan Son Nhut Air Base. Cargo container-sized pallets of beer filled a paved area the size of half a football field. Case after case, six-pack over six-pack, can upon can, America was putting together what was needed for an extended, successful campaign. Or so we believed.

In reality, the mountain range of beer was a sign of inertia in the war effort, of dwindling morale among soldiers and escalating political problems at home.

I wonder now how much beer we left behind when we choppered out the last of our embassy staff in 1975, with local hangers-on literally hanging on to each bird's landing gear. And I wonder how much beer veterans have drunk since that day to forget what they saw in the only war America has ever lost?

I had drunk too much beer myself, unfortunately, on the eve of the mama-sans' famous chicken cookout. I awoke just before noon with more of a desire to empty my stomach than put something else in it. And I knew I'd find Peter Ward's unwarranted optimism even more insufferable than usual.

Ward was the one who had inspired this idea, as he was always kidding around with the mama-sans. "You cook, you cook," he had urged more than once after giving them food he'd brought back from the mess tent or something he'd received from home. "You make meal for us some day, okay, Mama-san?"

"Okay, GI, we cook," they always agreed, though most of us thought it was just a running joke, like the one in which we accused them of actually smoking the Salems we gave them for their labor. "You like chicken, GI? We bring dish from home. You like." But one morning they did arrive carrying a basket of vegetables, a small bag of uncooked rice, and chicken.

Now, of course, when they had proposed "chicken," I had some vague idea of a soup or maybe, being a Midwesterner, a casserole already prepared. I foresaw them laying out a picnic, not roasting over an open fire.

That wasn't the worst of it, however. The first I knew that the long-promised dinner was a genuine prospect was when a live chicken ran through the hootch at full squawk. That's what woke me into a semi-nauseous hangover. A hen had squirmed out from under mama-san's arm and made a break for freedom, perhaps knowing that the sizable knife she had somehow carried through the checkpoint was intended to separate her head from her body.

"Hey!" Peter Ward said energetically as he spread his arms to frighten the hen back in the other direction. "There's no escape for you, my little chickadee." He laughed boisterously as he ushered the main course back toward the cook.

"Wake up, Landon," he insisted, clapping me on the shoulder. I sat on the edge of my cot. "Mama-san is laying on a feast."

My response, nonverbal, was graphically unenthusiastic.

"You just need some hair of the dog!" he laughed, holding up the beer he was drinking and pushing me toward the door.

Our two housekeepers were preparing to cook outside over a fire banked in the sand which surrounded our hootch. A five-foot high wall of sandbags surrounded the building, standard defense against the occasional mortar shells and even less frequent, but certainly dangerous, rocket attacks.

I arrived at the hootch door just in time to see mama-san behead the runaway hen with a swift chop and then turn her loose to run for as long as she could. When the poor girl careened along the sandbags, blood marked the wall with a line of squiggles. I wondered if there was a message written out in some script I couldn't read.

Neither this event nor the subsequent plucking and disemboweling brought the contents of my stomach up, but I did have to fight the impulse. I would not be a gracious initiate into the fine points of Vietnamese

158

cuisine that day, pretending to eat while consuming only a few sample bites.

Ward was characteristically enthusiastic: "Better than what we get in the mess tent, isn't it, Landon? Let alone field rations. Eat up!" He tried to fill my cup again with a greasy stew, bits and pieces of who knew what bobbing to the surface.

While she cooked, mama-san had explained what she was doing--things went into a pan, sizzling and popping--but with her pidgin English and my limited interest, little remains in my memory at this date. All the time they worked I found myself remembering what others had told me: the Vietnamese eat dogs.

I assume that accounts for the short life span of a GI's pet, that and an occasional shooting by either side (myself included). Young men with guns will find targets, I'm afraid.

Sending a rocket-propelled grenade into the side of a water buffalo is an even more horrendous prank, but I heard of it happening in the field more than once. Americans, long used to gasoline-powered engines, had no concept of the value of the water buffalo to this economy. The very survival of a family--or a village--is often dependent on the health of water buffalo.

These beasts of burden grow to great size and are trained to work hard, especially in rice farming, where they plow knee deep in mud. They like to wallow in the dirt and water much of the day, so rice fields are a natural habitat. Their great strength make them a match for a native lion or tiger--but not, of course, an American R.P.G.

We would have flinched at the thought of West frying. But exploding a water buffalo was just an amusing diversion for a slow-moving convoy making its way through the Vietnamese countryside. Must I say it? What asses we could be!

XX.

At home that night, a dull ache lingering in my jaw, I planned to dump my troubles on Bella, chief confidant and reliable source of sympathy. She would hear the sad tale of the Banister scheme and offer me relief, I thought. It didn't turn out that way. First came a typical brother-sister argument.

"He nearly got Taz killed today!" screamed Jenny as soon as I came in the front door.

"She was supposed to have him on the leash," Nelson countered.

"Wait a minute, wait a minute. Calm down now and tell me what happened. Bel, do you know about this?" She was coming out of the kitchen, wiping her hands on a dish towel.

"I came home in time to see what could have been a terrible accident, but I can't say who's responsible."

"He opened the door and let Taz out."

"It was her turn to walk him, and I assumed she wasn't such a dummy as to let Taz go to the door without the leash."

"Okay, okay. There was some miscommunication. But Taz looks--and sounds--fine to me." He had announced my step on the porch with his usual outburst and now was inspecting his bowl.

"He barely missed being smacked by a minivan," Bella explained. "Mrs. Thompson was on her way to the supermarket, but she hit the brakes just in time."

"I'm the one who caught him," asserted Nelson. "Miss Soccer Star was too slow."

I intercepted Jenny, who was ready to escalate from verbal conflict to physical blows, even though Nelson outweighed her by fifty pounds. "Whoa! Let's not get out of control. The dog's fine, no one has to be responsible. Just be careful, both of you, in the future."

This was hardly a stroke of diplomatic brilliance, but a refusal to lay blame, endorsed by Bella, was eventually accepted.

"There was one funny thing," she told me after the warring parties had gone their separate ways. "Taz scooting down the sidewalk when I jumped out of my car and scared him back."

"Ah, so you're the one who saved the day."

"I wouldn't say that, but my turning up just at that moment was fortuitous. What's so funny is Taz. You know, I've always thought he was a short-legged dog, low to the ground."

"Yeah?"

"Yeah. But I was always seeing him straining against the leash, getting as low as he can in order to drag whoever's walking him forward, toward where he wants to go."

I laughed at that picture. It was accurate.

"But when he had no leash on--which hasn't happened outside since he was a puppy, I guess--he sprang up to his full height. He's not short-legged at all. He was gliding across the ground on these long limbs!"

The picture amused me again. When I imagined him stepping in front of Mrs. Thompson's minivan, though, the sight wasn't pretty. He'd have sailed across the pavement, smack!

Smack. The image of flattened dog stayed with me through dinner. I felt it might introduce my confession of worries to Bella later. But she pre-empted me with her own concern.

"Do you know why I wore your old uniform when we stayed a night at the Coral Court?" We had just gotten into bed.

"Why? I . . . um . . . we already discussed this."

"I put on your uniform because I wanted to talk, Mark, about when you were in the Army."

"I probably need to go over that, too." Great, she was going to open up the chance for me to discuss Vietnam and the Banisters. "A lot of memories have been coming back lately. I've wondered if what I did over there made sense."

Even as I said this, another fleeting image passed through my mind. It was not a picture from my own experience, but something Warren Stevens had told me about from his travels in-country: Nui Ba Den--Black Virgin Mountain--a monument of stone and earth.

"When you were down to a few months in your tour . . . "

"A double-digit midget!" I interrupted.

"Less than 100 days left, right. I can't remember exactly when, but in the spring, I think, I went with a number of other graduate students to a weekend conference at Wash U."

164

She meant Washington University, the private school on the western edge of St. Louis proper. It's sometimes called the "Hilltop Campus." From its main quadrangle you can look down across Forest Park, the city's largest, and east toward downtown.

"You stayed there overnight?"

"No, we all went back to our campus, but the sessions ran from midday Friday to late Sunday. The theme was something like 'Is there a Self?' It questioned traditional notions of identity, automatic assumptions that we both have and can know our being."

"Sounds way too serious for me."

Again, the picture of a Vietnamese mountain, described by Warren, loomed in my mental scenery. Nui Ba Den is near Tay Ninh, close to the border with Cambodia. It was an enemy stronghold, even though it lay within South Vietnam's borders. A famous enemy staging ground was also close by, in the "Parrot's Beak," an extension of Phnom Penh's countryside poking into Saigon's.

"I don't remember any of the papers from the conference. That's not what I need to tell you about."

"You didn't write to me about it, so far as I can recall."

"No, I was too . . . too upset."

"Upset at a conference? I thought you academics were always cool and objective at such things."

"It wasn't the conference itself; it was walking from the parking lot to the conference hall."

This didn't give me much of a clue about how she'd been traumatized. Warren's description of Black Virgin Mountain returned. He'd been doing a story about village electrification in Tay Ninh Province, one of the central tenets of pacification. If we gave people in the countryside a better way of life, they wouldn't be good recruits for the Viet Cong.

"We'd had a long climb up from the parking lot, lots of steps to reach the level of the building. As we reached the top and started across open ground, we came upon a protest. People were chanting, some held up signs, there was a speaker on a platform."

"Anti-war?"

"That's right, though I'm not sure they were students. It could have been another group. And they did seem older, not like the college students I'd known back in Virginia."

"I missed out on all that, I guess. I wasn't paying much attention before I was drafted. And once I'd come home, I didn't want to think about protesting. It was someone else's problem."

Warren's first description of Nui Ba Den had focused on its natural beauty and its place in tradition. He made it seem like a mountain retreat, a place where pilgrims climbed to ask a holy man the secret of life. (I was ready for such a place now.)

The Vietnamese worship family. And it was thought by some that the spirits of their ancestors resided on that mountain, which, they say, is an imposing sight. It stands out alone in the region, almost a symbol of the people, their earthly home.

"All we wanted to do," Bella explained, "was go past the protesters and get to our conference. But we kind of paused at the top of the stairs, getting our wind, I guess you could say. And the protesters turned on us."

"Turned on you? What do you mean?"

"Because we were dressed up for our meetings, they took us to be some sort of officials. We were taken as war supporters or fans of the military, I don't know."

"Well, I hope you were a fan of at least one soldier," I chuckled, though I recognized this was not a laughing matter.

"That's what got to me. Someone called out, looking right at me, 'It's your fault people are dying over there. Your boyfriend is a cold-blooded killer.'"

"Hey! That wasn't fair."

Warren told me the U.S. could never dislodge the enemy from Black Virgin Mountain. They strafed it, dropped bombs on it, put down napalm. The Viet Cong held on, and we weren't willing to send patrols there because losses would have been too high.

"Of course, it wasn't fair. She had no idea if I had a boyfriend or where he was. But still . . . it bothered me. What did it mean that I had taken no stand on this war, that I'd just retreated into the graduate student's life? Was the war right or wrong? What should I have done that day, or after?"

"I . .but no words came out of my mouth.

"I didn't know myself, so I just ignored it, then forgot it. Went on with my student life. Waited for you to come home. The rest, I guess, as we say, is history."

History. But not a history I had ever recognized.

168

Interlude

During the spring before my Vietnam experiences came to the surface, coinciding with a mild mid-life marital crisis, I contemplated a cultural clash not unlike America's venture into Southeast Asia, one of Europe's post-colonial territories. It came back to me again after Bella's surprising account of her reaction to anti-war activists at Washington University.

The earlier revelation had come on weekend vacation. After a short visit with the grandparents in Fairfield, we took a float trip down the Cutt River. As too often happens, however, the expedition hit a series of snags, literal and figurative.

Characteristically, I had forecast a leisurely drive in moderate temperatures, a pleasant drifting with the current that required little effort on our part, and an elegant picnic on a sandy bank under the shade of magnificent Missouri oaks.

Instead, our car's air conditioner conked out 45 minutes from Fairfield (we were too far to turn back). The river, fed by heavy rains, was muddy and swift. And the mosquitoes dined far more sumptuously on us than we did on what was left of our supplies after two spills in white water.

Fortunately, the kids later made the day's disasters into a hilarious narrative, one of their happier joint ventures. And Bella was inspired by what she learned from the small-town outfit that organized our recreation. She drew from this Missouri history a moral for the Landon family I have treasured since.

I'd known vaguely about The Trail of Tears before this spring, but I learned much more at this occasion. In the last century, Cherokees were forcibly relocated by the government from native territory in Georgia to the grasslands of Oklahoma. Their sad journey went through Tennessee, Kentucky, the southern tip of Illinois, Missouri, Arkansas, and into Indian Territory. But it had never quite sunk into my consciousness that one route of their travel went through Phipps County, where I'd grown up.

"They came all sorts of ways up from Cape Girardeau," said Lester--of Lester's More Better Boat Rental. He and his family rented canoes and john boats, transporting vacationers from the end of the trip back to the parking area. They started midmorning and were back in their cars just before dark. "Some walked, some rode, some came in boats up the Arkansas River. There weren't no one path for 'em, but a lot did go by way of Springfield."

"I see," said Bella, who seemed to be more interested in this history lesson than in helping me herd Jenny and Nelson into the canoes. I was eager to get going, but she preferred to pause. Perhaps that was because she was already worn out from the heat in our unairconditioned car. "When was that, after the Civil War?"

"Nope, before. I think it all started in the 1830s, about then, well before the railroads reached this far west. Some Indians didn't want to come, of course. So it took the Army to move 'em out." Lester parked his broad behind on the dock railing, clearly in no hurry to launch us on a journey we'd already paid for.

"It's such a sad story," said Bella. "Women and children, the weather, sickness. What was it, over 1,000 miles?"

"Sure, especially when you figure it ain't no straight path. I forget how many died along the way. But you can imagine how hard it'd be, to lose your homeland."

"We tend to think all Indians were the same," added Nelson, taking an unexpected interest in adult conversation. "But the Plains Indians had much different lives than the

171

forest tribes. And the pueblo people farther west had other cultures."

When did he learn this, I wondered? Could it be that teachers are actually making students learn American history? I thought that practice had gone out with my generation.

"The Cherokee would have moved through different cultures themselves on the Trail of Tears," said Lester. "From their mountain land across the hill country of Tennessee and Missouri out to the prairie, which probably looked like the moon to them."

"They also had to put up with new laws and customs, the white man's way," added Nelson. "Even though they were supposed to have autonomy on the reservations, schools and churches sponsored by the government were teaching mainstream values."

Ah, now I saw it: he was identifying with the powerless. He and Bulk Order were the Indians; the Bureau of Indian Affairs was run by Bella and me. Of course, there's a small matter of perspective here. Parents are controlling, but that's hardly the same thing as an oppressive military power subjugating adults.

"Another thing," said Lester. "Along the way, some people took the usual advantage of the Cherokees--charging illegal fees to cross their land or to camp; selling food at outrageous prices; offering trinkets for valuable furs or woven goods. The worst was selling them liquor, which they drank and got rowdy on. Then, the law stepped in and roughed them up some more."

"How easy it is for us to forget that part of our history," said Bella. "It's like slavery. We pretend that, once it was outlawed, there are no more consequences. And we act as if the plight of the Indians was something that happened in another country, involving people completely unrelated to us."

"We hunted the buffalo almost to extinction," Jenny chimed in. "And the plains Indians had built their way of life around those huge herds roaming all the way to the Rockies."

"You can tell where the Cherokees walked," said a woman I've assumed since to be Mrs. Lester. She too leaned on the railing.

"How is that, ma'am?" asked Nelson. I have to admit he even asked politely, the way his mother had tried to teach him.

"The Cherokee Rose. Whenever a mother on the Trail of Tears wept, her tears turned into a flower."

"A rose?"

"That's right. The heart of the white flower is golden, reminding the Indians of the gold that was found on their land in Georgia. Of course, that's what attracted whites and eventually led to their being driven off-- simple greed for gold."

"Can we see roses on our trip?" Bella asked.

"You can. They have seven leaves, which is the same number as the clans that went on the Trail of Tears. And they grow all along the way."

"Okay, let's get ready," Bella ordered. And now we put our supplies in the two canoes and prepared to start the trip. My earlier urgings had been ignored.

"You watch along the way," said Mrs. Lester, handing Bella a postcard picturing the Cherokee Rose. "It's a high climbing rose, got a lot of thorns. You can see it, almost like a hedge."

Later, I would read that another meaning of the "Cherokee Rose" is the mixed-race children born along the Trail of Tears. Some

174

stayed with their fathers and grew up as members of the white community. To the Cherokee who went on, however, this generation was lost to their own nation.

In the calmer moments of our float trip-- and, happily, there *were* a number scattered among our mishaps--I thought more about the Trail of Tears. But I didn't connect it to another route of migration until Bella's confession of her doubts about the Vietnam War the following fall.

If one branch of the Trail of Tears crossed Phipps County and continued toward Oklahoma, it had to follow more or less the path of the later Route 66, Ralph Banister's highway. Lester had said they passed through Springfield, a straight shot from Fairfield. America's Main Street was laid, then, on top of the sorrows of earlier residents, Native Americans. On the tears of the Trail.

In the late 1920s, civic leaders and business interests in the states from Illinois to California got together to map out a transportation avenue from the center of the nation to the West Coast, a route to prosperity. The road they proposed was an expression of countless citizens' desire.

The Trail of Tears, however, was a path no one wanted to travel. It was the imposition of a destiny on one people by others who had more power.

I fear America did--or, rather, tried to do--much the same thing in Vietnam. We wanted another people to walk our walk, talk our talk. It was as doomed a venture as the forced migration of the Cherokees was a tragic one. I didn't see it at the time.

Nor did I see it fully when Bella told me about the incident at Washington University. Too much was going on all at once in my life for me to assemble this truth and come to terms with it.

Bella, bless her, had always been farther along that road than I was. As we were driving back to the grandparents' house in Fairfield, she articulated a moral from the day: "Our troubles are molehills," she said to us all. "Molehills compared to the mountains of sorrow endured by Indians on the Trail of Tears."

My testing in Vietnam was small compared to what many others endured. And some 58,000, of course, did not survive their trials.

Volume Three: The March.
Chapter XXI.

Soon after Taz's brush with death in the form of Mrs. Thompson's minivan, Bella proposed that the two of us go away for a few days. She wanted me to confront my participation in the Vietnam War. She also hoped to examine her own tacit endorsement of that campaign. I resisted, of course.

Bella proposed Mary's Peak, a retreat in Missouri's St. Francois Mountains. "Western has used it for years," she explained. "They take couples or larger groups. The idea is to get away from the confusion of daily life and gain perspective." The St. Francois Mountains rise in groups of two or three peaks to the west and south of St. Louis County in some of the most rugged land in the state.

"You know how I feel about mountains." We were talking on the phone, as she had stayed late at her office for evening meetings with students. Because of classes there was no other time for some appointments.

"Yes, but you're not going there to build a road. You have to admit, we're so busy here day to day that it's hard to find an extended time where we can get beneath the surface."

In one way, I realized, this might be the logical place for me to piece together elements of my past. I had once lost--and then recovered--fundamental coordinates of my existence traveling not too far from the St. Francois range. It was also not distant from the Banister farm in the Pacific region.

On childhood trips to visit my grandmother back East, I had once seen tall caves opening into limestone cliffs beside the road. For a long time I believed they were located beside another highway, the one we took from Fairfield to Jefferson City, the state capitol where my father's parents lived.

It was, however, on the way to my mother's mother in New Jersey, traveling Route 66 into St. Louis, that I had spotted what turned out to be the work of a gravel company carving rock out of the hillside. One summer during my college years, I realized the error I'd made.

I had been pleased to get the axis of my home state's geography straight again. But I've always remembered this early confusion of east/west and north/south as a bad sign for a future highway construction engineer!

I tried another tact with Bella. "We're getting into the holiday season. We don't have time." While the phone was at my ear, I hoped also to hear Nelson pulling into the driveway. He'd been out with the band practicing, I guess. "Thanksgiving, Christmas, it will be busy." I remembered my dental schedule, too: the first session with the endodontist was next week.

"We can plan for early in the New Year. My semester doesn't start right away, but our two kids will already be in class."

My work should be calmer then, too, though I wasn't positive the Banister land matter would be resolved. An escalating range of meetings still dominated my images of the future.

"I don't really believe in retreats," I reminded her. "It's just an excuse for a holiday. You get all warm and fuzzy, but it doesn't solve any real problems."

Her response was sharp. "You understand that you're dismissing a principal tenet of my profession?"

"Not necessarily." She'd caught me there, so I tried to give ground by referring to another situation. "I do remember a case in Vietnam where people might have stepped back to look for the big picture."

179

"Oh? Well, tell me about it tonight. I've got to run now. But I'm going to ask about Mary's Peak tomorrow. It's important."

I pretended I would look at schedules when she got home, though I also knew I would have an excuse to forget if Nelson and I had another argument. His latest scheme was to skip his senior year of high school in order to play music. A guidance counselor-- some idiot!--had told him he already had the courses to get into college. With decent SAT's, why, he wouldn't need a diploma.

I'd always opposed the idea of children skipping grades, leaping over one of the regular steps in development. No matter how smart you were, I argued, you had to climb the ladder of years by putting a foot on each rung. Bella had always agreed, pointing out the need for gaining social skills and physical maturity to rise to new challenges. But this time, adding to my irritation with her, she wasn't automatically opposed to Nelson's idea.

Nelson and I avoided a clash when he came in, though. I was calling out for pizza with his favorite toppings on half (he'd recently gone vegetarian) and what Jenny and I would want on the other. I did insist the three of us sit together at the kitchen table, as a family. He accepted that idea, and

180

conversation skimmed politely along the surface without creating waves.

When Bella came in, Jenny was watching a knitting show on public television and Nelson was abusing his African drum upstairs. "You see your students?" I asked. I was loading the dishwasher, hoping to put our disagreement out of sight as well.

She lifted her satchel by its shoulder strap and let it thump onto the floor beside a kitchen chair. Then she sat down heavily. "Yes, all done for the day. Well, except for looking at these files for tomorrow." She gestured toward her satchel.

"I have to work a bit myself later. Another position paper on the road project. After all we'd done in planning from an engineering point of view, now I have to rethink everything with a view toward history, toward a Route 66 tradition."

She kicked off her shoes and motioned toward the refrigerator. I knew she wanted a glass of sparkling water, so I reached into a cabinet for a glass.

"You were going to tell me about how people in Vietnam could have stepped back and found the big picture?"

"Oh, yeah." She was supposed to have forgotten. "One of the guys I got to be friends with over there was an Army reporter."

"He was in your unit?"

"No, Warren Stevens was with Army Headquarters, in fact. But he traveled around doing stories all sorts of places. He did a couple of real good pieces about our unit, about engineers."

"Were you quoted?" She smiled, taking a big sip of her drink. I took that to mean she felt I deserved some recognition.

"I might have been. Anyway, what was I thinking . . . ? Oh, yeah. What I recalled when you were talking about getting away from it all was what he told me about military command."

"The people who were in charge of the war?"

"Well, in charge militarily. Nixon and Laird and those guys back in Washington made the big decisions. The politicians."

"But your friend, Stevens, he learned something about the top brass?" I chuckled at her use of the term.

"He saw them. See, back in Long Binh, where Army Headquarters was, there was a regular office complex. Warren told me it looked almost like a college campus, a quadrangle surrounded by concrete buildings."

"I guess I know what that looks like!"

"But you probably didn't see it on television back home. I don't think we wanted people to realize how large our presence was then. Nixon had to start bringing down the troop level not long after I came back so America wouldn't think the war was taking so many men away from home. There was an election coming."

"What I remember you telling me about is wood barracks, with mostly screen walls for ventilation, tropical style."

"Um-hmm. Our hootches. Anyway, back in the Long Binh office complex, they had meeting rooms, places for conferences. Warren told me about a briefing room where they showed television news coverage from the States."

"Makes sense. They would want to know how the war was playing in Peoria."

"Yeah. I guess it was one of those studios, a dark room with rows of seats like in a movie theater. But the mistake they made was this: they clipped together all the evening network news stories on the war, one right after the other. Then, they'd play them and watch. Here's NBC, then CBS, ABC. And a lot of nights it was one bad thing after another."

"Bombing Hanoi and Haiphong, body bags, napalm. I remember seeing those pictures. It wasn't encouraging for us."

"Warren said it wasn't encouraging for them either. But part of the problem was they were so close to it all. When they watched those unfavorable stories all spliced together, they couldn't get any distance, any perspective."

"I see what you mean."

"Of course, our colonel always talked about successes, how well it was going." I paused. "But we didn't always feel it."

"So, you had doubts? You questioned the effort even while you were there?" She took a long sip of her drink. Then she said, "If we don't get away to talk about all this, I seriously wonder how we're going to keep on functioning as a couple."

XXII.

Driving to work the next morning, I thought some more about how we are so often overwhelmed by the details of everyday life. When you struggle dawn to dusk with a variety of little problems, it's hard to separate the important from the trivial.

For the past fifteen years, I'd done the reverse: rather than bunching all my regrets and sorrows about Vietnam together, I'd spread them out so far from each other that I didn't confront a single one.

The words "Operation Freeway" rose out of the list of unhappy events from my year of service. "Not ready for that one," I said to myself and concentrated instead on the scenery.

I was passing through the I-44/I-270 interchange in Sunset Hills. The ongoing effort to gather basic information for the department's position paper about rerouting the interstate was taking me today out to Eureka.

To contest Ralph Banister's argument about preserving a section of old Route 66, I would have to review the different paths the highway had taken since its inception. That meant, among other things, consulting records in a number of municipal and county buildings in St. Louis and the surrounding area.

Having wandered through many a paperwork maze for previous projects, I knew my day would likely be frustrating. As a matter of fact, the cloverleaf interchange I was (trying to) move through might have been a model for my research journey.

The westbound lanes were reduced to a single strip of asphalt on what had formerly been paved shoulder. The department was working on the old lanes to my left, and I knew this path was only temporary. But the two former lanes could not handle current rush hour traffic, which bottlenecked approaching an old bridge just past the interchange.

As I crept along, I considered the military's strategy for giving my engineering company breaks from difficult assignments-- the 15-day standdowns after 45 days in the field. Back at the base, we were supposed to get some distance from the actual operation, its dirt and grime and danger and frustration. We were to return with a restored sense of the mission's goals.

That's when we had our occasional hootch parties. Many nights we also went to watch the Filipino rock bands that put on shows at the enlisted men's clubs. Since their music was recycled American rock-'n-roll, rhythm-and-blues, and some country and Western, we were often able to disengage our brains from the daily routine. Of course, a steady flow of Falstaffs also helped us slide into relaxed, nostalgic musings of home.

The single-file row of cars I was following pulled onto the bridge, whose surface was also being worked on in anticipation of new damage from winter cold. We moved even more slowly across that expanse.

There was a steady but low-level ache in my jaw from the bad tooth. Testing it with my tongue, I felt that the gum around it was swollen, too. I would be glad once this was fixed.

Of course, when bands played, soldiers always wanted the singer, if there was one, to do a striptease. As with any group back home, the male backup musicians had their synchronized steps and the female lead had ways of accentuating songs with some version of a belly dance. Generally, though, she wouldn't strip.

Occasionally, however, one woman, somehow knowing no one in charge that particular night cared, would respond to our urgency. The process usually started when a soldier close to the stage stood up between numbers and led the crowd in a chant, "Take it off, take it off!" The rest of us would cheer and clap, at first only halfheartedly because we expected to be disappointed.

Often, the instigator would pass a hat around and we'd each throw in scrip, a dollar or two. He would offer the hat to the girl, but when she reached for it, he'd pull it back and insist on clothes coming off. The rest of us would chant louder, pound our fists on the tables, whistle and yell.

At last I passed over the bridge and back onto the main highway. Traffic was gradually speeding up as it left the bumpy temporary paving and spread out onto two good lanes. I would be in Eureka in another few miles.

This kind of driving was frustrating, of course, and I doubted if Ralph Banister's children and grandchildren really wanted to see a return to 1950s style of travel, as represented by his section of old highway. In those days, stretches of open road alternated with town streets that featured a stoplight at every corner. There had been no limited-access bypasses around big cities or business routes that took Sunday drivers out of the way of through traffic. You were lucky to average forty miles per hour on a long trip.

If the first call for a striptease captured the consciousness of the crowd and generated widespread pleading, the band's leader might signal to the other musicians. The game was on. The drummer and the bass would establish an erotic beat, and the singer would start to gyrate to that rhythm. *Boom-pa-ba-boom, boom-pa-ba-boom.* The guitar decorated the *ba-booms* with deep rich chords.

These interstates weren't built because engineers wanted something to do. It was drivers who demanded shorter travel time and easier driving conditions. Americans want to push the speedometer to seventy-five and not have to touch the brake pedal going from St. Louis to Kansas City.

The nation's leaders back in the '50s knew from the experience of World War II that efficient transportation of weapons, military supplies, and troops made us a more powerful force in the world. Ralph and Sarah both acknowledged Route 66 had aided the war effort because it was a sophisticated and efficient pathway for transcontinental traffic.

Of course, there were good and bad dancers on American bases in Vietnam. When the merely mechanical performed, GI's kept their focus on drinking. But they responded to singers/dancers who were subtle and controlled in the steady swing of their torsos and only occasional hip thrusts, the traditional bump and grind. The one I remember most vividly, Star, danced calmly for half an hour at exactly the same pace and never removed a stitch of cloth. Yet, she brought a club full of men to a point of frenzy.

I saw a school yard on the south side of the highway and what looked like a new building under construction. Again, I was witnessing suburban growth--people moving from the city--but also newcomers from the counties further west who wanted to take advantage of the city. They came for professional sports, major shopping centers, better schools.

The model to me for what was happening here was northern New Jersey, where my mother had grown up. Across the river from New York City, each town had grown until it met its neighbors. So when we used to drive from my grandmother's to visit an aunt and uncle who lived three towns over, we never encountered countryside. It was all one metropolitan expanse.

The expression on Star's face never varied, though she seemed to look directly at each of us. It was probably an illusion, but I felt that she understood our needs. At times I was sure she had singled me out, her eyes locking with mine through the thick cigarette haze. In a tight red miniskirt and halter top, she had--or she was--a heavenly body.

While other band members asked if we wanted her to strip, Star stayed in one place with the microphone on a stand before her. The drummer called out to her, though we couldn't hear what he said. The bass player leered as he strummed. The guitarist pointed to the hat filling with money.

In time with the drummer's continuing beat, Star bent one knee and the hip on the opposite side rose, bent the other knee and the other hip was lifted. Up and down, side to side, over and over, her pelvis rocked as we stomped our feet and groaned with the music.

Every half a minute or so, after a cycle of this gentle, regular *boom-pa-ba-boom, boom-pa-ba-boom*, Star gave her behind in its tight red miniskirt a spectacular ride. It took a semicircular journey out and around a perpendicular line running from the top of her head to a point midway between her feet. To the left her rump went, then way out back

191

behind her, and finally around the right went this sexy woman's behind. When it returned to its starting position, Star's red bottom landed with a sweet erotic bump.

And, in a related orbit, out from our bodies traveled the confused hearts of men far from home. Aching with love for the ones we'd left behind and sore with longing inspired by a dancer from another world, our spirits revolved around the sadly fixed point of our present place in the universe.

Interstellar gravity tugged us by our heartstrings, and sometimes we wept.

XXIII.

"Okay, look," I said to Bella a few days later. "Maybe I do need to open up about my Army days. It's long enough ago now. But you don't really feel our marriage is in trouble, do you?"

We were getting ready for church. I sat on the edge of our bed while she held an outfit up in the full-length mirror beside the door to our bathroom.

"Mark, I don't think you see how you're acting these days. You're moody, short with the children, especially Nelson."

"Oh, I think that's all pretty standard father/son stuff." I recalled how I'd battled my own father the summer before I went off to college. In one of my angrier moments, I'd smashed my fist through the wall of the stairway up to my room.

"You keep trying to get Jenny to say she'll devote her life to soccer. Daughters always want to please their fathers, and she's too young for that kind of pressure. She needs to explore other interests. This embroidery is a wonderful outlet."

"All right, all right. I'm . . . I'm trying to keep my distance on that. She's a girl, and I can't put myself in her place." I paused. "Still, she plays so well!"

Bella snorted. "See! There you go, ignoring what you ought to understand." She bent down to find the right shoes in the rack on the closet floor.

I had stopped getting ready at the point of needing a tie. I don't wear ties as a rule, unless I'm meeting with legislators or presenting at community meetings. I had two racks full of Christmas and birthday present ties to choose from, but sometimes it was hard to pick.

There were other reasons for my being stalled in getting ready. Dressing for church on Sunday morning was often a hump in the flow of the weekend for me. A lot of times I let Bella and Jenny go without me. Nelson, of course, had refused to attend once he started 10th grade.

Ironically, I often enjoyed a modest sense of satisfaction after the service. It was not that I felt reassured of heaven hereafter or anything like that. I guess it was the traditional rhythm of the Episcopal prayer book that settled me down.

Bella suddenly spun around to confront me. She was more heated than I had thought. "Don't you see that you're not always very pleasant to *me*?"

This startled me. I felt I was always pleasant to her. What was she saying?

"We're pretty typical of old married couples. I mean, when both are working, there are a lot of demands. And teenage children." I knew, though, when I thought about it, that I had shown irritation recently at her having to be at work so much, especially on nights and weekends.

"I guess I need to remind you again," Bella insisted, "that counseling is my profession. I study this sort of thing all the time. Relationships--college students dating, couples, family dynamics--that's what I do!"

I stood my ground. (Well, I sat it, I guess, still on the bed.) "Yeah, so I build roads, and that's not always easy."

During the last few days I'd begun to wonder if I was really going to win the battle with Ralph Banister. Strange people had gotten involved in the debate--local historical societies, certain small businesses, tourist boards. It was all getting to be a tangle.

"I don't think I'm getting through to you." Now Bella was shaking a finger at me. "Sure we struggle in our jobs, and that creates friction between us. That's normal; we can deal with it. But you're also blocked at some point in your past. Maybe it's not just the year in Vietnam, but something specific that happened. I've always wondered why you never contacted any of the men you served with once you were home again."

Then I remembered, "Bill Pierce and I agreed we'd get together. I didn't realize he's a veteran, but he said he'd like to talk. And he gave me a book to read. I *am* doing something."

I pushed up from the bed, expecting this announcement to end discussion. Bella continued, but perhaps a little less fiercely.

"That's only a first step. You need to come to terms with Vietnam. Then, you need to come to terms with me. I believe you'll see that we need to get away."

"To learn about me as 'soldier boy'?" I sang the phrase in the style of the 1960's hit by The Shirelles, trying, desperately perhaps, to lighten the mood. She sighed and turned back toward the closet.

"You continue to forget *me* as the war bride, Soldier Boy. Though I wasn't technically even a fiancée yet, I realize now I was going through a hard time while you were away. That's a big part of the equation."

I knew this was true. Bella's first year of graduate school, I'd come to understand, could be as much a concern as my year overseas. But I may have been afraid to know more of her story.

Jenny called up the stairs that she was ready, and this brought our exchange to a conclusion. Still, I hoped I could avoid packing off to Mary's Peak and a weekend of soul searching. A few nights at the Coral Court, now--that made sense!

In the meantime, I did have that beer--or two--with Bill. We met in Park's, a steakhouse with a bar. Bill had proposed Park's after church the previous Sunday, as it wasn't far from his office and I was generally on the road these afternoons after doing research somewhere.

"You won't believe how I lasted through the last weeks of my tour," he told me. He was perched on a stool at the end of the bar. I was next to him, but my stool was placed so I could play a pinball machine, "Rocky Road."

"Your final 100 days! I suspect it involved drinking plenty of these," I nodded at my glass of Michelob, but kept my hands on the buttons that worked the game paddles.

"Well, I did that too. But what kept me sane was building a Stratego set."

"Stratego?"

I glanced up at him, though I also tried to watch my ball and the scoreboard. The object was to propel balls up a rocky road, between two mountain peaks, and into a plush valley.

"A war board game. Ironic, of course. Playing a child's war game in a combat zone!"

"Maybe I do remember Stratego. Tell me about it."

"There are two armies run by the two players. Each guy puts out his pieces--offense and defense. You also have to hide a flag, your headquarters. I made the board and all the pieces out of heavy cardboard. The pieces are standup L-shapes with symbols drawn on the front sides, the Stratego logo on the backs."

"Oh, wait, I do remember. Your opponent doesn't know if you're placing bombs or troops. He just sees the back side. If you attack bombs with one of your units, it's destroyed. But if your firepower comes up against a smaller force, you win."

"Right, and the idea is to blow up the other guy's headquarters."

I was using my hips to bump the pinball machine, helping the silver ball bounce off trees, stay out from under waterfalls, avoid avalanches. Every ball that reached the mountain valley earned me 10,000 points, but smaller scores could be rung up by avoiding caves or sinkholes and ricocheting off obstacles.

"It's all in placing your pieces, as I remember," I told Bill. "He has to read your mind and guess if you're surrounding your flag with troops or bombs." *Hey, ball! Not off the cliff!*

"And sometimes the flag is unprotected, but in the last place anyone would think."

Taking a long drink before loading the final ball, I wondered if I had hidden my flag, the secret of my wartime crises, from Bella. Perhaps I'd even hidden from myself my own headquarters.

"You tell Mary about your experiences?" I nudged the pinball machine with my pelvis again. *Stay on the path!*

"Yeah. I've told her a lot." His wife was an emergency room nurse, so she probably wouldn't have been shocked at much, even though she was younger than he.

"I've never talked much about it, to Bella or anyone."

"Not a good idea, Mark. These things get bottled up, and they affect other parts of your life."

"But that hasn't happened to you." I bumped the machine.

"Oh, yeah, it did. I was blocked. Couldn't think about it, wouldn't talk about it. And I'd get depressed, drink too much."

"But, didn't you just say you've opened up with Mary?"

"Mary's my second wife."

"Oh."

"Janet divorced me two years after I got back. She couldn't put up with the drinking . . . and what would happen later."

I humped the machine. *Shoot! Tilt.*

XXIV.

Bill's revelation about his Vietnam-inspired depression bothered me. Bella had said I was blocked. And, much as I had resisted her assuming the role of my counselor, as well as the idea of a weekend's confessional retreat, I was beginning to think she might be right. I couldn't move beyond some moment in my past. Still, I wasn't sure I could tell *her* about Operation Freeway. And certainly not about Frank Middleton.

During the next week, though, my attention was diverted again to the battle over highway construction. I received an unexpected call from Ralph Banister inviting me to meet him Friday at the old high school in Pacific. He had something he wanted me to see.

I was sure this was another ploy to argue the value of old Route 66. America's Main Street had passed right through Pacific and, I assume, in front of the school. But it couldn't hurt to continue to be friendly with Ralph, especially if, in the end, we had to take his house and land. Too, it was a beautiful day to be driving west from the city, not a cloud in the sky.

Ralph wanted me there right at noon, so I figured I might be able to take him out to lunch--if lunch could be found in Pacific, which had lost business to faster-growing communities nearby and to the big malls on the west side of St. Louis.

I'd always liked this little town, which spreads out in a flat valley among high hills. The Meramec River, fed by a spring close to Fairfield and traveling toward the Mississippi near St. Louis, runs south of the town. Cliffs rise up on the other side of the river, and the country down that way is pretty rugged.

There's one great stretch of level, straight highway, though, the old Mother Road running parallel to the Missouri Pacific tracks east toward St. Louis. If I sight down that line, it almost makes me think I'm in the western part of the state.

Ralph was waiting for me on the sidewalk in front of the school, along with several dozen other people. At first I thought I'd been ambushed: this was going to be some demonstration he'd organized to protest the new highway. Then I realized everyone except Ralph was facing away from me and toward the high school building (actually now converted to a condominium). They were watching someone in the parking lot.

"You're just in time," Ralph told me. He took me by the elbow to join the crowd viewing a tall man in a cowboy hat beside a white pickup.

"What's going on?"

"Tumbling pigeons. Ever seen them?"

"Tumbling . . . ? No." My mind ran through ideas of homing pigeons, messenger pigeons, pigeons in the park. I'd never heard of tumbling pigeons. The man in the hat was opening wooden cages in the cargo section of his truck. These must be the tumbling pigeons, whatever that meant.

In a hushed voice, Ralph was explaining. "Most people in this county think of pigeons as a nuisance. Especially in urban areas, they're always on the street pecking at food dropped by residents, or at garbage. Sometimes people feed the pigeons. You know, grandfather and granddaughter on the park bench."

"I guess I've done that myself. So, are they going to hop over each other, or do somersaults on the sidewalk?" I tried to peer over shoulders to see if the birds were jumping off the truck and onto the parking lot. But no. With a whoosh the birds, out of their cages, soared up and away in a flock. We all watched them, some folks letting out a soft sigh or small gasp of satisfaction at the birds' flight.

"They do their tumbling in the air. You'll see."

As the birds rose up to several hundred feet and swept in an arc toward the south, out over the Meramec River, I realized I'd seen this many times in the past. Most small towns, just like cities, have their resident pigeons, and they're frequently seen soaring above stores and office complexes. If there are wild pigeons out in the world's forests, I'd never heard about them or their habits. Town pigeons I knew.

Fairfield's flock, as I remember, roosted on the Phipps County Courthouse and could be seen getting regular exercise by flying from that hilltop location out over the town. Our pigeons would sweep east out over the high school, north across the campus of South Central Missouri State College, west above the hospital, and south along the edge of Fairfield cemetery.

While the spectators in front of the former Pacific High School watched these birds, Ralph told me more. "Tumbling pigeons were first bred in the Middle East as far back as a thousand years ago. It's a genetic trait, passed on, of course. And certain pigeon trainers kept tumblers or rolling pigeons as a kind of specialty."

"It looks to me as if these birds are flying the coop," I said with a chuckle.

Ralph laughed, too. "Oh, no. They do fly high and pretty far, but they'll come back across this spot a number of times. Bert Overstreet--he's the trainer--knows what he's doing."

I could see Mr. Overstreet talking to a handful of interested persons who'd stepped up from the crowd. He gestured off in the distance to the west, shading his eyes against the bright overhead sun.

I asked Ralph, "Why is this all happening today?" I still wasn't sure this wouldn't turn into a demonstration against the project.

"He does this about four times a year, just for fun. People in the area know about him, and word of mouth usually gets a nice crowd out for the birds."

"Um-hmm. Sarah's not here?"

"No, she's with our daughter and grandchildren in Tulsa for a week or so."

"But you didn't go?"

"Look! Here they come."

From the east came the flock, perhaps 200 yards up and in a fairly tight bunch. Then, all of a sudden, it appeared as if a third of them had been shot. Their wings folded up and they fell down through the main group, making it look, from where we stood, as if they were dozens of torn bits of papers dropped from the sky.

"Whoa!" was all I could say. And before I articulated a concern that they were goners, the tumbling pigeons unfolded their wings and flew back up to the join the larger group. The same thing happened on several more passes.

"Pigeons can tumble or roll," Ralph explained. "Some do somersaults in flight, head over heels. Others dive and spin, as fast as thirteen revolutions per second."

"Wow! Why in the world do they do it?"

"We're not sure. It's genetic, as I said. Bert's explained the 'ro' gene to me, but I don't understand it completely. I thought it was some survival or escape mechanism, dodging predators. But he says it has to do with chemical processes inside the bird. They speed up the production of essential material, enzymes or something especially important to metabolism and flight."

Again, the tumblers dropped from the formation, fluttering and flipping in brief free falls before righting themselves. "Are they all tumblers, trading turns, or just some of them?"

"Only some. The others are a kind of base. They'll lead them home after a while."

"Oh, so he doesn't have to call them down to these cages?"

"No, they head back all on their own. When he gets there--it's about thirty miles south of here, over those hills--they'll be settled down, a happy flock."

As he spoke, the birds made what would be their final pass above us and then swung out across the Meramec. The performance was over.

"Ralph, that was great. But why did you want me to see?"

"I just thought you would enjoy it. I know you've been working hard, as I have, though we're on opposite sides of this road issue."

"I regret that, but I don't see that I have any choice. Our transportation system has to expand to handle the traffic. We need a bigger road."

"Ah, yes. But those tumblers--aren't they great! They're not just rushing along like everyone else, racing to get on with things. When they free-fall like that, I sense an unfettered joy. They drop out of the pack, but they're not really loners, not isolated beings. They have their special identity, changing the pace. And they bring the rest of us such pleasure."

He was a subtle one himself, this fan of old Route 66. He was a tumbler, spinning away from the pack and blurring the outlines of the formation. I just hoped he wasn't getting too many other pigeons to go with him.

XXV.

That night I was drinking a cup of coffee at the kitchen table while Bella cleaned up after dinner. Jenny was working on a small piece of tapestry up in her room, but at least she'd participated at an informal practice of the soccer team that afternoon. Nelson had gone out somewhere.

"I've made a temporary reservation for our retreat," Bella said.

"My schedule's pretty full." She gave me a dark look. "But I'll see what I can do. When are we talking about?"

"After New Year's, the same time I've mentioned before. The kids are at school, but I'll have a flexible schedule."

"Um-hmm. That might work." Of course, I still hoped that her enthusiasm for this project would cool between now and then. "Do you know where Nelson went?"

"Jamming. He says Bulk Order's sounding pretty good. But, by the way, they're going to change the name."

"To . . . ?"

"Well, they're not sure, but the leading candidate . . . now, this is what Nelson says, so don't be angry with me. The current name is Big Daddy's Road Hog."

I sighed. "And you think that's directed at me?"

"Not necessarily. But he does think you're crowding him, and he's heard all that complaining about people who stand in the way of progress. So, maybe . . . "

She had stacked the last of the dishes in the dishwasher and was putting on rubber gloves to wash pots.

"Let me remind you that I'm not the only one involved in this project," I said, a bit more stridently than I'd intended. "My whole department agrees that we have to put the road through Banister's land. And all the higher-ups at the state level have known about this for months."

"I know, I know. But you'd been visiting the Banisters, telling me how nice they were. The perfect grandparents."

"Well, I do like them. It's just that in this case they're being unreasonable."

"Unreasonable, hmm. I suppose that could be so." She had piled pots, pans, and lids in the drying rack on the counter. She seemed to pause, looking at the window above the sink. Then, she went on. "Well, on another topic: I've been pretty busy with student appointments lately, and many of them have to be in the evening."

"I've noticed that." I'd prided myself on not complaining.

"I was thinking . . . perhaps there's something I could do . . . being nervous about coming back home so late."

"Oh, I don't think it's too late for driving," I pointed out, thinking that's she'd been home by 10:30 at the latest. And that was only a few times.

"Yes, but still . . . it's awkward. Anyway, there's something I might do . . . . You see, Western has some efficiency apartments for faculty and staff, just one room with a kitchen at the end. And a bathroom, of course."

"Yes?" I was not taking it in.

"So, anyway, I can spend the night there sometimes. I mean there's one that's empty, and the Dean said she could leave it unoccupied for me. Just those times that I need it. You folks here can take care of yourselves for one night."

So, there it is. Flat out of nowhere. Worse than separate beds or my sleeping on the couch. Perhaps even a neat little step toward divorce itself.

But, wait: don't overreact. It might just be a threat, a warning. Best, for now, not to make too big an issue of it.

"You have to be the judge." I set my coffee cup in the sink. "At the moment, I've got highway documents that need my attention." When I sat down at the rolltop desk I had in the corner of the living room, I realized my day couldn't be getting much worse.

At lunch Ralph had roused the dog of war one more time. We were at the Diamonds Restaurant in Villa Ridge, not twenty miles from the scene of tumbling pigeons.

He hadn't rattled me with any more references to the joys of traveling down old Route 66 than was indirectly implied in his praise of tumbling pigeons. But the old guy had somehow drawn an unhappy admission from me that I was much farther than I thought from coming to terms with my past-- and with my son.

"Tell me about your time in Vietnam," he'd asked while we waited for a waitress. This single-level, light red brick building with wide windows, by the way, had once claimed to be the largest roadside dining establishment in America, I guess during Route 66's heyday. Not far from Pacific

212

(where, Ralph said, with the Red Cedar Inn closed, we'd have trouble finding lunch), it was still a major interstate truckstop.

Of course, like so many businesses that had once enjoyed thousands of cars coming right up to their front door, it now sat back off the main road and had to lure its customers off the expressway and up a service road in order to survive.

"My time in Vietnam? Oh, pretty routine, I think. I was one of the lucky ones. Twelve months as a combat engineer, little contact with the enemy."

"I see. So, it's more psychological damage than physical damage in your case?"

I didn't think there'd been damage in any lasting sense. After all, since that time I'd advanced steadily in my career, maintained a marriage, raised--or nearly raised--a family. I was hardly one of those troubled vets you saw on television--unstable, suffers flashbacks, prone to violent outbursts.

"When I returned, I went on with my life pretty much as I'd planned. I've wanted to be an engineer since I was boy. Always loved to build things--kites, roller derby cars, shelves and cabinets for a refurbished stationwagon. With a friend I even turned an old garage into a little store for neighborhood kids."

Our waitress brought our drinks and sandwiches. Ralph unrolled the paper napkin that held the silverware. "But you engineers struggled with projects in Vietnam, didn't you?"

"Yes, that's true. Sometimes it seemed we were spending more time tearing things down than building them up."

A jungle scene flickered in the back of my mind, a memory of some operation. It was the view I had from atop my Rome Plow.

"You were part of forward operations?"

"A few times. Not good times."

"I've read about that. Clearing landing zones could be especially dangerous."

I looked around the restaurant, which was perhaps half empty, not much of a lunchtime rush. I didn't think weekdays would be better, as there wasn't a large local crowd in this rural area. The road brought customers, or there weren't any.

"Is there a reason you're not with Sarah down in Tulsa?" I asked. "Didn't you say there were grandchildren to spoil?"

"Yes, I am missing that . . . for business. You see, I've become kind of a celebrity around here as an after-dinner speaker.

214

Maybe I should thank you for that." He chuckled.

"Oh, yes. Preservation, Lions Club, historical societies. Well, it's good we're debating these things."

The jungle scene became more distinct in my memory. This was not a regular day when we worked to expand or maintain an established open area around known villages and well maintained roadways. We were going into a district we'd never worked before. That's why what I recall is dense jungle--giant trees so thick they almost made a wall.

"It's a hard thing to decide," Ralph went on, "what to save, what to let pass. You Vietnam veterans have had a hard time figuring out what to keep from your experience. Should you remember any good times, or would it be better to hold on to the difficult truths so we can apply them in the future?"

"Damned if I know!" I was surprised at my energy. But then, I realize the scene I'm recalling is from Operation Freeway. I almost hear that woman's scream.

"Do you talk to your own son about what you did over there? He's the next generation, of course, and probably needs to know what you learned."

At that moment I realized for the very first time: I'd never said a word to Nelson about Vietnam. Had I wanted to spare him? Or was it, once again, me I wanted to protect?

At home that night with Bella, I tried to avoid explaining what Ralph and I had talked about. Not many days ago, I'd wanted her to share my frustration with his "save the old highway movement." Now, I was trying to avoid questions from her about what should happen to his section of Route 66. I knew she'd turn whatever was said into another reason we should go to Mary's Peak. And I was running out of excuses.

XXVI.

On paper, a root canal is a straightforward procedure. At least that's what I believed as, sitting in Dr. Hartman's office, I read the brochure I had been given by the receptionist.

The endodontist, according to the flyer, first numbs the area surrounding the dead tooth. Then, he (or she) drills a hole into the crown. Inserting small files through the hole, he cleans the pulp out of the interior, including the root extending into bone.

After the pulp is removed, the endodontist fills the hollow center of the tooth, usually with gutta-percha or another malleable substance. The hole in the crown of the tooth is then filled, or the tooth is fitted with an artificial crown. Presto! Good as new.

Why, then, I wondered, as I found myself again tipped backwards in a dentist's chair, did Dr. Hartman want to insert this rubber thing (a "dental dam," she called it) so far back in my throat that I was on the edge of gagging?

To be honest, I was uneasy even before the dam (which, I was later informed, was to prevent anything falling down my throat). As soon as I realized Dr. Hartman was a woman, I wondered if it wouldn't be better to back quietly out of the office and reconsider the whole matter of my sore tooth.

Not, of course, that I assumed Dr. Hartman was incompetent, poorly trained, or anything like that. It's just that I hadn't expected it, hadn't prepared myself beforehand.

My generation assumed all doctors (and engineers) were men, all nurses and secretaries women. We'd learned intellectually that this wasn't always the case, but, without being forewarned, these stereotypes could still govern our expectations.

Dr. Hartman's manner, at least, was reassuring. "I'm not doing anything you haven't had your regular dentist do," she explained. "I'm basically drilling and filling."

"But Bill said he wouldn't take this on," I pointed out. This was before the dental dam was inserted, obviously, or all I'd be saying was "*Ahg, nuhg, ahg.*"

"Dr. Pierce couldn't do the root canal nearly as quickly as I can with this special equipment. In addition, I've not only had all the dental training he has, but additional training in this specialty. It's what I do; it's all I do. And I'm good at it."

I considered Bella's expertise in counseling. She, too, had done both graduate study and clinical work, passing examinations at school and board certification afterwards. If I knew how good she was at her work, I shouldn't question this endodontist.

Still, I couldn't help being a little troubled at my helplessness. My feet were higher than my head, my mouth was stretched as wide open as it would go, my arms were wrapped in an apron (and couldn't have let go of the armrests my hands were gripping ferociously anyway!). This woman and her assistant, who was occasionally suctioning saliva from my mouth, could do pretty much anything they wanted to me in this vulnerable position.

When Dr. Hartman produced the dental dam, I wondered what else the little brochure had failed to mention about the process of performing a root canal. I didn't have to wait to find out.

"You're going to experience some unpleasant odors here," Dr. Hartman informed me. "The tooth contains bacteria, necrosis. And I'm opening it . . . right . . . now."

I don't think I'm the kind of person who would smell death just because someone told me it was coming. But at that moment, my nostrils were suddenly filled with the stench of disease and decay. Since I couldn't say anything except "*Ahg, nuhg, ahg,*"--which I did say--I opened my eyes wide to underscore my discomfort and my unhappiness.

"This isn't too bad," Dr. Hartman observed to her assistant ("Melinda"; I saw the name stitched on her scrubs).

It made sense, of course, that this tooth, which had been hurting on and off forever would be damaged. It's insides had been slowly souring or rotting for who knows how long.

Dr. Hartman either didn't see or deliberately ignored my distress and kept working. She put aside the high-speed drill and asked her assistant for a number 52 something and a number 57 something else. I could hear a high-pitched rasping sound as she scraped out the inside of my tooth.

Making a mental effort to distract myself from what was happening, I reconsidered the idea of a weekend retreat with Bella at Mary's Peak. Maybe it wouldn't be so bad, after all.

On another issue, perhaps in the end I'd lose the debate with Ralph Banister and

220

friends about highway improvement and have to go back to the drawing board for the whole project. I suspect there is a route I could follow, a mere twenty or thirty miles out of the way. It would mean seeking extra funding and incredible delay, but I'd still be employed at the same salary, wouldn't I?

Suppose Nelson skipped his senior year of high school. He was a smart kid and would do fine at any public university. Northeastern Missouri State was only a couple of hours away, and it wasn't so big he would be just a number. If he screwed up, at least he couldn't blame his old man.

Jenny might decide to devote herself to embroidery. What did it matter to me? If women's athletics was a suddenly rich field for someone of her abilities, there were no doubt other areas in which she could distinguish herself. One day she'd seize a different opportunity unavailable to previous generations.

Surely this tooth must be empty by now! I think the Novocain is wearing off, as I can feel the end of each file poking into the base of the tooth. Or is that bone she's jabbing? "*Ahg, nuhg, ahg,*" I think to myself, no longer believing that vocalizing my concern will change the course of events here.

I try to go back into a "march" mode.

That's what I called the frame of mind that allowed me to last through two years of military service, one year of it in a combat zone. The march mode involved mindlessly walking forward, one step at a time, doing the next thing that had to be done.

This wasn't something I mastered immediately upon induction, of course. Those unhappy days of early training had inspired plenty of chafing, angry letters home, a few nights of excessive drinking with others in my company. By the time I had orders for Nam, though, I'd discovered the virtues of "the march."

The ability to march comes when you resign yourself to the fact that you have no viable options other than the one you've already taken. You accept the huge construct of values and tradition into which you've been born and let it dictate your daily routine, even when it threatens personal integrity. (Later, you come more and more to wish you had found an alternative.)

Was this a war you had volunteered to fight? No. Was it a war the nation's leaders believed was necessary to protect our way of life? Yes. Did your father and his father and your ancestors take up arms in similar situations? Yes, they had. Could you in good conscience plead the status of a pacifist, dodge the draft, or flee to Canada? No. Why, then, do you feel so guilty?

Whatever the final judgment on your decision, you can acquire an unanticipated power of endurance that has plenty of subsequent application. Work as a civilian, for instance, was never that hard after my time in the military. Any roadblocks, detours, and delays in my career were never quite as odious after I had been chosen, by whatever forces rule this universe, to survive danger and return home. Others, of course, had not survived or returned horribly broken.

"Your tooth's clean," announced Dr. Hartman. She'd been making some sort of progress report all along the way to Melinda, but I hadn't understood the terms they were using or read their expressions above their masks. I couldn't determine if the process was going well or descending into complete failure.

"*Ahg, nuhg, ahg?*" I asked, wanting to know if she could finally remove the rubber shield that had been crammed to the back of my throat. I was beginning to think if she waited much longer, I was going to remove it along with the contents of my stomach.

"Now, we just do an impression, put the temporary crown on, and we're done for the day."

Done for the day! I wanted to be done forever, but Bill had said several sessions. Surely none would be as bad as this. Or so the brochure seemed to imply. I returned to march mode.

Dr. Hartman spread a cool jelly over the hollowed tooth and its neighbors. I then had the pleasure of sitting for what could have been five minutes as that goo in my mouth set. I also still had a dental dam in the back of my throat.

When she prised the mold loose, I began to relax. Unfortunately, she also wanted an impression of the teeth below the dead one, I guess eventually to ensure my bite was straight. My ordeal of the day had one more phase.

I knew, of course, I would survive a root canal. I didn't know if I would survive a divorce.

XXVII.

I went home ready to accept the idea of a weekend retreat at the beginning of the new year. But I didn't have time to get the acceptance out of my (sore) mouth before Bella stunned me with a new, unexpected bombshell.

"Nelson's moved out." She met me on the front porch, having thrown a dishtowel over her shoulder, as she often did when preparing dinner. I heard Taz's customary barking behind her.

"Out? Out of his room?"

"Out of the house. He's moved in with Preston Waite. That garage apartment he has behind his parents' house."

Preston's folks were well-to-do, a fact which encouraged me to conclude that their son the guitarist had been spoiled from an early age. The Waites lived on several acres out in the country, and the second floor of their spacious garage was a two-bedroom apartment. Bulk Order (whoops! Big Daddy's Road Hog) practiced in an area at the back of the first floor, which had not been converted from its garage status.

"I'll go get him right now." I turned around and headed for my car.

"I hope you won't," she called. I looked back at her, that towel now clutched in one hand, anxiety on her face. She must have been watching for me from the kitchen window, wanting to catch me the minute I got home. But why? To stop me from rescuing Nelson?

"What! Let our son ruin his future by doing drugs in some dive with a high school dropout?" I felt like flinging my briefcase into the bushes. Why was I working so hard if my own children didn't give a damn about what we did for them?

"No, I just mean don't go after him right now. Give him time to figure this out himself. You're too worked up to act rationally. Come inside and we'll talk."

"Oh, I'm the one who's not rational! Yeah, that makes sense, perfect sense."

But for some reason, I was willing to hear her out. I stormed past her into the front room, depositing my coat on the back of a chair and my briefcase at my desk.

"You've been under a lot of stress," Bella said, following me. "Now's not the time to do anything hasty."

226

I marched toward the kitchen to fix myself a drink. I could see what was happening. It was taking some time to absorb, perhaps, but now I understood: this house was getting ready to empty itself of everything and everybody but me. Bella to her college's efficiency apartment, Nelson to Preston's. When, I wondered, would Jenny decide to move out and enroll in a boarding school for advanced needlework? And how about Taz? He would probably slip his leash and go off to live in the woods, a wild, long-legged dog in a growing pack.

Why, in fact, was I staying myself? I should ask Ralph and Sarah Banister if I could move in with them, especially as they'd stay right where they were while Interstate 44 begged for a route in other counties--or another state. Let's all move out!

Drink in hand, I strode toward my usual living room easy chair. I felt Bella watching me from the kitchen door. She'd checked on the stew I'd seen simmering on the stove.

"I had a call from Bill Pierce today," she said quietly.

"Bill? About my tooth? I was at the endodondist today. First phase of the root canal is all done." I tested the soreness around the tooth. Actually, any tenderness seemed primarily to have come from the Novocain shots, not the procedure of drilling and scraping.

"No, Bill thinks . . . he thinks you're . . . that you need to get some things out in the open. Talk about the war."

The war! Great. Now he's joining the campaign to institutionalize poor crippled, psychotic Mark Landon! Why doesn't everyone see I'm doing just fine?

"Well," I said, adopting an ironic stance without quite knowing why. "Well, I did think maybe I could use a hobby these days, a way to relieve the tension."

Bella sat on the sofa. "Now that's a good idea! You used to jog. That was good for you. You ran several of those 10K races. Are you going to take that up again?"

"No, I thought I'd try something a little more sedentary, but also more intellectual." I took a long sip of my drink. Would she have a glass of wine? Sometimes she liked a white or a rose. "I've been thinking about what Jenny's doing, with her sewing. And where, for her, it's kind of self-expression. Pre-teen self-examination. I guess, I thought it might be calming for me."

"I see." She was understandably cautious in her response, eyeing me.

I went ahead, unfairly cocky, potentially mean. "Look here now: embroidery is an ancient, ancient art. Decorating the Tabernacle in the Old Testament, that Bayeaux Tapestry about British history and all, making curtains and upholstery in early American homes."

"True. There's a long tradition, especially in Western culture. But you've never shown an interest in women's work."

"Maybe there are things about me you haven't noticed. For instance, I've learned there are certain basic stitches in embroidery, but countless variations." I'd skimmed one of the magazines Jenny had left on the coffee table, and all this was really just coming off the top of my head. I took another long sip. I would soon be ready for a second Scotch.

"There's the flat stitch, a knotted stitch, and . . . what was it? Oh yes, the loop and the chain. They're all different, but you can use them to develop a complete picture, a whole landscape if you want."

"And you're going to do embroidery, then?" I could tell she didn't believe me, but she wasn't sure why I was going on.

"Well, I'll have to fill up the time evenings and weekends." I paused. "When there's no one else in the house. Nelson the rock star has left. You're the all-night campus counselor."

"Oh, that's not going to happen very often. But, still, now that you mention it, it might create some space for you . . . to think things over, to find a way to go forward."

"My being blocked, of course." I heaved myself up from the easy chair. "Of course, I can always fill up some of my time with a second or third drink."

She got up from the sofa and followed me to the kitchen. "You don't need another drink. Call Jenny, and let's have dinner."

"I don't need to eat. I want to devote myself to crewel work, or works of cruelty."

"Mark, don't be ugly. Let's just eat now, and we can talk more later. You have to go forward. You can't let all this fester."

Well, damn it; it was festering. I knew it. Everything in my life had backed up behind some gigantic roadblock--my career, my marriage, my family. I had come up against a wall named Vietnam.

Vietnam had once been in my past, behind me, over with, I thought. But then, it had somehow run around me and popped up in the future, directly in the pathway to tomorrow. I had to find some way beyond it, or through it, or around it. Everything that mattered to me was going to grind to a halt otherwise, but knowing that didn't help me figure out what to do next. And the easiest thing seemed to be to lash out.

"Hey, I won't bother you. I'll be out of the way. Just go on about your life as if I wasn't here. That's apparently what I'll have to do, as you won't be here."

"You're deliberately misunderstanding. This is my job now." She paused. "And I certainly might sleep better those nights."

"Oh, you're sleeping fine. You're certainly not keeping me awake."

She hesitated. "Mark, it's the other way around. Your dreaming is keeping me awake."

"Dreaming? Well, even if I am, that shouldn't affect you. All *that* goes on in my mind, you know."

I hadn't said anything, but I had been having a lot of dreams lately. One in particular.

"I know you're the only one who sees the dreams, but . . . "

"But . . . ?"

"But you talk. Or moan, rather."

"I do?"

"You must not remember in the morning. I often just nudge you, or say something quietly. Sometimes you startle, but then you go back to sleep."

"Not every night? Not enough to force you out of the house?"

"I hope that's so." She sighed. "And, of course, I couldn't leave Jenny."

XXVIII.

You'd think, if I was actually haunted by my experiences in Vietnam, I'd have dreamed about Operation Freeway or Frank Middleton's death. But I didn't. Those events, I guess, were locked in reality and wouldn't be transferred to dreams or anywhere else. What had been occupying my nighttime consciousness, oddly, was processing.

Processing, of course, occupies--or seems to occupy--a tremendous part of your time in the military, especially if you're enlisted personnel. Induction, training, transfer, assignment, release--all involve mountains of paperwork and eons of waiting.

These were the phases of my long ago Army career that dominated my present subconscious, my dream landscape.

Now, it's true that most of the dreams I was having at this time placed me in Vietnam, but not out on an operation. Instead, I was at some permanent base trying to complete the paperwork necessary to get to, or get back to, my unit.

Occasionally, my subconscious, no doubt influenced by events on the evening news, sent me not to Vietnam but to Central

America. At least once I found myself in an undetermined African country. And I vaguely remember being in Eastern Europe, in a Slavic nation where the rough guttural language of the natives and a swirling snow of deep winter overwhelmed me.

Most often, the scenarios into which I was thrown, no matter what the location, were not remembered events but new experiences, familiar in general but in none of the details. Usually, I found that I had been called up again for active duty and then shipped precipitously overseas, the result, I always assumed, of some sudden development in a distant part of the world to which I'd failed to pay attention.

Maybe that's what made me so sad during the dream and when I awoke: I knew from the start that I had done all this once before. And I realized how pointless much of it seemed in the end. Now I--as well as, presumably, thousands of others--had to do it all over again.

Many times, I was with a bunch of young recruits. Retaining my middle-aged identity, I felt confident that I knew what was coming and that I had strategies for coping. But the same didn't apply to my companions. These raw kids, wide-eyed and uncertain, reminded me of what I had been decades ago. They were innocent where I was experienced, trusting as I had turned cynical, hopeful against my fatalism.

"Do you hear that thunder?" one blond eighteen-year-old would ask his neighbor, perhaps someone of Puerto Rican descent.

He responds, scanning the sky above the mountains, "But there's no cloud." Should I tell him it's us, our planes, steadily bombing distant targets? No, they'll learn in time.

As the dream continued, I'd move with a stream of replacements through a tin-roofed Quonset hut set on sun baked sand. A typically silent supply sergeant would hand me stiff, new jungle fatigues. I jammed everything into a deep duffle bag, comfortable with the knowledge that they'd soften in use and suit the tropical climate we had entered.

There might be the issuing of weapons and other combat gear, though not as it had happened with me, in fact. I would sling an M-16 over my shoulder in a familiar gesture, holding with my other hand an ammo belt heavy with full magazines. I accepted the helmet and the flak jacket and the grenades without comment, even though, in real life, I had been in the direct line of fire for the tiniest fraction of my time in-country, and that at considerable distance from an unseen enemy.

There were insurance forms to fill out (who do you want to be your beneficiary? [*should you be blown to Kingdom Come over here!*]); options to mark on government forms for receiving pay (U.S. Savings Bonds kept for you back home? [*or automatic deductions for the spouse and children you might never have*]); medical records to be verified (check here if you received explanation stateside about the prevention of malaria, the danger of venereal disease, the cash benefits payable upon the loss of one limb, one eye [*two testicles*]).

In between all the steps of moving from station to station in-processing were more instructions, additional questions, the endless filling in of blocks on government forms, and long, long stretches of waiting. Sitting on a sandbag wall, leaning against the side of a tin hut, stretching out on a wooden floor, I listened to the newbies worry about their next 364 days.

"You volunteer for this?"

"Not me, man. I'm going to keep my head down, do my year, get back home."

"Yeah. Me, too."

How little they foresaw what lay beyond the dangers they could imagine. Out there in the future, I saw their possible deeper disillusionment with the system, brought out especially if they returned to an ungrateful home population.

Would they be for years embarrassed at their service in a cause that history later deemed futile and perhaps misguided? Would scenes of returning World War II era GI's, bending girlfriends back in deep kisses and showered in the ticker tape parades of big cities, underscore the absence of ceremony at the end of the present conflict? Would another generation struggle to justify what they'd done in the war, Daddy?

Perhaps worst of all in my dreams of processing would be the futile effort to get to the next stop in some complex itinerary, attempted transportation in stages toward a distant goal. Rather than finding each effort a positive step toward that fixed destination, I repeatedly discovered myself moving farther along a path that led in exactly the wrong direction.

I might know I was supposed to report to a master sergeant who was directing troops to their new units: infantry here; artillery there; engineers somewhere.

"Take this packet to building 21-14, other side of that mess hall, around the corner," some personnel officer would tell me, thrusting into my hand a manila folder full of ditto sheets held together by a metal clasp-- my orders, I assumed.

"The mess hall . . . ?" I would ask, seeing a row of wooden buildings all alike, the words painted on the little signs at their entrances blurry and unreadable. Did any say "21-14"?

But I would start off anyway in the direction indicated, naively confident that I had been given all the necessary information. As I passed a building or spotted a landmark or turned a corner, nothing like building 21-14 appeared before me. Instead, I found a deuce-and-a-half parked, its motor idling.

"You going to 21-14?" asked the truck driver, who had been watching me approach through the open window. "Hop in."

Hitchhiking on bases was routine, and any jeep or truck would stop for a GI's raised thumb. So I climbed into the truck bed, happy to have run into someone who knew where I was supposed to be. I sat sideways directly behind the driver, leaning back to peer around the truck's cab.

"Thanks," I yelled up to him, as he ground the gears and gave the engine gas.

238

Then, desiring, I guess, a sense of camaraderie to balance the assembly line nature of processing, I'd try to start up a conversation. "Sure is hot!" I called, catching his eye in the side view mirror.

"Oh, you get used to it," he called back, grinning.

Soon we were speeding past warehouses, slowing around Vietnamese pedestrians with bundles under their arms, grinding up to a helipad where the noise of choppers landing and taking off was deafening. But where the heck was building 21-14?

"Did you say 21-14 was close?" I shout over the roar.

"I'll put you off at the corner. Follow those guys."

I saw a dozen grunts walking slowly along the side of the road. They were saddled up and covered with dust.

"They're going to 21-14?"

"No, they're going out again, but they'll point you to it."

I fell in at the rear, realizing that I wouldn't want to walk far with a full duffle bag slung over my shoulder, heavy parts of an unknown weapon dangling from my fist.

"21-14?" I ask the young infantryman beside me. When he turns to answer, I see Nelson's face, but more tired and sad than I've ever seen it in real life.

"*Ahg, nuhg, ahg!*" I exclaim. In my dream-turned-nightmare my mouth is dry and I cannot form words. I want terribly to speak to Nelson, to say his name, to tell him everything he should know to survive what is to come. "*Ahg, nuhg, ahg,*" I cry louder, but no more clearly.

The troop in front of Nelson turns around, perhaps at my mouth's working and its gasping, groaning sounds. I'm shocked a second time. It's Jenny, her beautiful young face marked by dirt, grease, and--can it be?--blood.

XXIX.

The next day my jaw swelled up. With a lump the size of an apricot in my cheek, I had to put on hold any decision about Nelson, our son who had perhaps run away from home.

I was inclined for the moment to let Bella have her way on this one anyway, hoping he would come to his senses without our threatening punishment we would probably regret enforcing. Bella agreed to talk to the Waites as a cautious first step, making sure it was okay with them that Preston had a roommate. She would also find out if Nelson was showing up at school.

I was on the phone to Dr. Hartman as soon as her office opened, 8:30 a.m., hoping she would dismiss this swelling as routine. "It's not that painful, but I don't look so good," I explained, my tongue a bit thick and slow.

Again, her voice, even over the phone, was reassuring, and I suddenly imagined how nice it would be if she, like the doctors of my childhood, made house calls.

"Put ice on it," she said. "And stay home from work today. Many times it's something you did in your sleep. Rolled on it; rubbed your jaw; even bumped into your spouse. Did you take one of the pain pills I gave you?"

I should have known I'd injure myself. However, maybe I could blame Bella for this. I was making her--or Nelson--responsible for everything else that was troubling me!

"Let's see: I did take a pain pill last night, but this morning I'm worried that it's an infection."

"Remember, I started you on an antibiotic, so that shouldn't happen. Still, we can't be 100% sure. Take your temperature every two hours, and call me around noon." I had taken both pills last night, just the antibiotic this morning.

Still, this could be exactly what I needed, time away from work and my increasingly compromised interstate project. I wondered if this whole tooth thing could be stress related?

"Thanks, Dr. Hartman. Again, I look awful, but I don't feel that bad."

"As long as there's no temperature or additional swelling, you should be fine. If things change, though, we'll squeeze you in between appointments this afternoon."

Okay, then. A day off for me, although it might be, after Bella left for Western, an unhappy preview of my lonely future. She would drop Jenny off at school on her way to Western, abandoning me to an empty house. Well, me and the dog of war. And in that case, I might be better off alone.

I was spared the empty house, though, when Jenny announced she didn't feel well. "Cramps," her mother whispered to me. "Just let her go back to bed. She'll probably be up and fine by noon. I've given her what works for me." I wished she had a pill for what ailed me.

Still, I took what I had: a day off. I refused even to think about Banister's growing list of allies: small businesses that wanted to develop a Route 66 theme; Chambers of Commerce that hoped to slow traffic speeding past their restaurants, motels, and souvenir shops; environmental groups that were opposed to any new development.

Instead, I started reading the book Bill Pierce had leant me, *Dear America: Letters Home from Vietnam*, a collection of correspondence from the war zone to family and friends back in the States.

After his divorce, Bill explained, he'd done a lot of reading. His shrink advised it. So, he researched the war and post-traumatic stress disorder. The experiences of other veterans, both when they were in Vietnam and after they'd returned home, had helped him put his life back together after his first wife left him.

This book, *Dear America*, apparently came later in his reading. But he'd told me nothing else had captured the shrinking sense of purpose GI's experienced while serving in Southeast Asia. The letters they wrote were so honest, so direct, so sorrowful that you felt you were getting the truth of history.

I wasn't so sure it would work for me, but I figured at the least it would be one step I could tell Bella I was taking to come to terms with my own experience. Since I tended to doze off after every dozen pages or so, anyway, as a result of my pain medication, it wasn't too wearing.

As I read, it occurred to me that this book offered something not all war writing did: absolute authenticity. History is generally written by the winners, of course, and those who survive often speak as if they had anticipated the outcome of events. Hindsight is the trick of prophecy.

But letters written on the scene, before the course of history is established, capture the uncertainty, the confusion, the doubt of those involved. In the Vietnam War those factors increased as time passed.

244

Early letters in the mid-1960s expressed confidence in strategy, a belief in the cause, the power of idealism. These soldiers were continuing the great efforts of their fathers' World II generation to battle totalitarianism. But by the late '60s, especially after the Tet Offensive of 1968, the tone of letters changed. Pessimism and cynicism had replaced patriotic zeal.

I took a break from reading and napping for lunch: a warm cup of chicken noodle soup into which I crumbled Saltine crackers. This was traditional invalid fare in the family and wouldn't, I thought, injure my jaw so long as I was careful.

Sitting at the kitchen table, I eased one more spoonful into my lopsided jaw just as Jenny came in. She was wrapped in a terry-cloth robe and looked kind of beat up herself.

"Want some soup?" The words were muffled, in part because my mouth was full of soggy crackers but also because of the swelling.

"No," she answered, frowning as if I'd deliberately made myself hard to understand. She leaned forward and looked in my bowl, then jerked her head away: "Phoo!"

But she slid into the chair opposite me, drawing her knees up under her chin and resting her feet on the edge of the seat. She scowled across the table. "You don't look like you should be eating, either."

"Still pretty bad, hmm?" I leaned down to inspect my reflection in the toaster, and even in that imperfect surface the one side of my face was obviously puffy--and it hurt now. "The dentist said I would be okay if my temperature didn't go up."

"Hmm." I suspected she wasn't concentrating on my problems. "I have a question for you, Dad."

"Okay." Almost any distraction from bad memories, stalled road construction, or toothache was welcome at this point.

"Why do I hurt?"

"Hurt?" She had caught me off guard. "Didn't your mother explain that . . . your cycle and . . . all." I dwindled off, not prepared for this subject, though I'd insisted on handling related matters with Nelson some years earlier. We had had several sit-down sessions and some follow-up questions and answers that convinced me I was performing my fatherly role with appropriate diligence.

"Yeah, but that's just talking about my body, biology and stuff."

I was puzzled: what did she want to know here? Not only was I poorly informed on the details of menstruation (blame it on the reticence of my parents' generation), but I had never given any particular thought to the mechanics of pain. All I remembered being told or reading was that pain was the nervous system alerting us to trouble. This fact inspired me to want the pain pill I had skipped this morning. The bottle was on the counter.

"Do you mean, why do you feel this way every month and some girls don't?"

"No, but now that you mention it, I do think it's unfair Jeannie doesn't have cramps and still has such a great body!" She said this with the first slight sign of energy. "Right now I feel like I've run into a brick wall!"

"But you're such a fine athlete, and you look great. Why, I'm already having to chase the boys away!"

I could see that this helped, as she managed a small grin. But it apparently wasn't a complete answer. She shifted in her chair, her arms still wrapped tightly around her drawn-up legs.

"What I mean is, why does anybody hurt? Why did God make us this way?"

Whoa! This was worse than I'd thought. I was in for a discussion of theology here: why does God, who is all powerful, not squash the fallen angel, Satan; why are there such things as sickness and death in a world He created; why does it rain on the just and the unjust, the well-endowed and the flat-chested? I was probably more ready to talk about a woman's period than this! Did I dare try the old standby, "Ask your mother"?

XXX.

Thank goodness I was saved by the bell!

"I'll get that!" I volunteered with an enthusiasm I'm sure had been missing from my side of this serious conversation. By "that," of course, I meant the doorbell.

Taz came racing down the stairs as usual, though he was a bit slow in the attack because he'd been sleeping on Jenny's bed. (He assumed that anyone home during the day meant he had the right to get up on that person's bed.)

The intruder wasn't the house call I'd contemplated earlier in the day--from the endodontist, Dr. Hartman--but it was close: Bill Pierce, my regular dentist.

Taz's outbursts were directed at people who were outside the house--in the street, on the sidewalk, at the door. Anyone already inside must be a friend. Since Bill had made it comfortably into the living room before being spotted, Taz soon trotted back upstairs to join Jenny in another nap.

"Let me take a quick look," Bill said, pointing to the easy chair I'd been reading in. He tilted the lampshade to redirect the light.

"You're going to tell me to say 'Ahh,' aren't you?"

"Yes, but gently. Don't pull anything that doesn't want to be stretched. Hmm, that doesn't look too bad. The swelling will probably go down by tonight. You're continuing the antibiotic?"

"Faithfully," I insisted. The engineer in me always made sure I followed instructions. "But I am due for a pain pill." I gestured toward the kitchen where I'd left the bottle on the counter.

"Good, good." Bill cut off the lamp and sat down on the sofa as I went to take the pill.

"Sit a minute, unless you're in a rush," I suggested when I returned. "If you've come out of your way this far, at least let me get you something to drink--coffee, a Coke?"

"No, nothing to drink. I just finished lunch." But he settled in on the sofa. "This is my afternoon off, so I can stay a bit. Now, if I played golf like all the doctors, you'd have been on your own!"

"Ha! You sure on the drink? I'm not putting much in my mouth, following Dr. Hartman's orders."

250

I gestured toward Bill's copy of *Dear America* on the end table beside him. "I have been reading the book you lent me."

"I see. Tough going in some spots, isn't it?"

"It is. Makes you remember stuff you hadn't thought about in years. I guess it's mostly the bad memories we sweep under the rug."

"And then walk the other way." Bill was tight-lipped.

"But little things, trivial things, they just slip away over the years, too. I'm not sure which this is, bad or trivial, but not long ago I suddenly remembered what burning human excrement smells like." Now that I think about it, my root canal may well have trigged this memory.

He had a puzzled look, and I remembered he'd been at Cam Rahn Bay, one of the biggest U.S. bases along the coast. They probably had a genuine sewer system.

"On the fire bases, I guess, where there were open latrines. They would burn them off. Throw on gasoline, drop a match. It's the darkest smoke and the sharpest smell I've ever known."

In my mind's eye it was a familiar sight. A group of Vietnamese workers was obscured by dark smoke rising. The shapes of small men with pale conical hats leaning on long-handled shovels stood out against a background of jungle. We often paid the people who owned this country to take care of our waste, though some poor GI's were put on this detail as well.

Bill nodded. "I thought at first I'd be separated from smells like that, from what we used to call so casually 'blood and guts.' I was basically a clerk, you know, a record keeper."

"But . . . ?" I felt there was more he wanted to say.

"Well, they were always short of personnel at the hospital, and now and then I was told to help out. Especially with head wounds, anything around the jaw."

"That wouldn't be fun."

"Not the sort of thing I was planning for my later life as a dentist--filling cavities, cleaning teeth, simple orthodontist work." He paused thoughtfully. "In Nam I saw too many men with too much of their faces gone. We all got into more than we expected."

In my memory, I was preparing to mount my Rome Plow and rip into the trees behind the Vietnamese civilians burning human waste. In Operation Freeway our commanders believed we would finally relieve a bottleneck for refugees seeking shelter in towns close to American bases.

"Let me tell you about this one situation," I said. "It was lots more than anyone expected."

The main route for a flight of refugees, I explained, wound down a river valley from the hills, twisting through a series of narrow passes before reaching the relative safety of swampy terrain. The Viet Cong routinely attacked villagers traveling on foot and any American patrols on operations in the vicinity.

The mountainous landscape meant choppers had to come in low to use their firepower, and that made them targets for forces dug in on the ground. Our troops couldn't get there in personnel carriers, or at least not very quickly. So combat engineers were asked to create a new road.

"We were good at tearing down forests," I explained to Bill. "We had equipment to chew up vegetation, level a hill, bridge a stream or even river. We were going to create a shortcut from the provincial capital to an area of threatened villages, A.S.A.P."

The easy part, building the road to where the land rose sharply, had been done by another company. But the stretch we had to work went through an abandoned rubber plantation, a remnant of the French colonial era. We were to carve a three-mile shortcut to the old road, with an especially difficult part between a swamp and a steep, rocky ridge.

"We knew the engineering part of it was a challenge, but we were ready for that. Unfortunately, we didn't see the human construction in our way."

Bill interrupted, holding a hand up with the palm facing me. "You're talking an awfully lot here. Is your jaw all right?"

"It must be the pain pill kicking in." I tested my mouth with a yawning motion. "I feel like it's actually loosening up. But that rubber plantation didn't loosen up a bit when we got into it!"

Even as I went on with my story, part of me stepped back and wondered: why was I all of a sudden launching into this tale? I wasn't just reciting it; it was pouring out of me. Well, that could be the pain medication, too.

I recalled the rapid advance we made in the first week of the operation. Not only did we establish a solid foundation, but we were also able to clear a lot of forest on both sides of the roadway, lessening Charlie's potential ambush sites.

For a change, many of us were enthusiastic about our work. It was like the road-building we had done or would do one day back home--more construction than destruction. Sometimes we even imagined ourselves traveling here--packed in the family car on summer vacation--rather than picturing the victims of war who would take this route beside carts loaded with the last of an entire clan's worldly possessions.

"Of course, what we had to work with, in laying down the bed, were maps and aerial photos and statistical data about the region. None of us really knew the land or the people who lived on it."

"I bet a lot of your information was out of date."

"There it is! We were building a road in a landscape of our own imagining, a fantasy world we thought we understood. The reality was much different."

I paused as a flood of images rose around me: smoke from burning piles of foliage; the roar, grumble, and whine of heavy machinery; rich smells of tropical vegetative life and the bite of gasoline; the bucking seat of my Rome Plow and the wrenching pull of its controls; continuous salty tastes of sweat and fear.

"What we saw as a stream to be bridged turned out to be a source of fresh water for tiny camps that didn't show on our maps. The buildings from the old plantation we assumed had been abandoned in the mid-1950s? Makeshift homes for half a dozen families of no particular political persuasion. And the hill in our way--through which we blasted a cut thirty yards wide--had hosted a marginal coffee farm for Montagnard people who had retreated from their ancestral homes to the north."

I paused and then admitted the worst. "And then, first thing one morning, we drove over a family. Dropped a forest on all but one poor woman who wished we'd taken her out, too."

Volume Four: The Road.
Chapter XXXI.

Mary's Peak was dangerously attractive. I felt myself relaxing immediately in the snug one-bedroom cabin perched on the side of a Missouri mountain. I know now, of course, that was exactly what Bella had intended.

We had come here before Christmas rather than wait until early in the new year. Bella had seemed particularly solicitous of my emotional state, especially as Nelson showed no sign of returning home and my anger had erupted in several ugly fits.

She had determined that our son was keeping up with all his responsibilities, just doing so from another base, the Waite's garage apartment. So, she said, let him work this out on his own.

I disagreed, arguing that we ought to make some things clear at this point. If he wanted to be free of parental restraints, for instance, he should start paying more of his own way.

"My grandfather left home to work in the coal mines near Helsingborg at age thirteen," I pointed out at one point. "But he didn't ask his parents to pay for music equipment."

"Those were different times, not to mention a different country."

"And there was mandatory military service in Sweden. Serving his country gave him a trade and eventually an income."

"Nelson's more fortunate in several regards, then. He can serve his country without joining the Army, and he has the support of a loving family."

I wanted to argue more, but I was afraid Bella would once again turn the topic back to me, the obsessive father. The more I fumed about Nelson, I'd learned, the more my anger, not its object, came under scrutiny. And, to use a military expression, I wasn't standing up under inspection very well these days.

I wondered if Bill had encouraged Bella to think of me as a troubled veteran. Though he assured me he hadn't repeated my account of Operation Freeway, at times Bella seemed to look at me as a man about to come unhinged.

I believed, though, that, if I was uneasy or thoughtful, it derived mainly from the root canal. While the swelling had gone down and I suffered no infection, there were three more appointments to face. Add to that ongoing ordeal worry about the highway project and general family problems, you can see why I moped from time to time. But, in part to avoid the charge that I was afraid to face these issues, I agreed to do the retreat early.

The view from the front of our cabin was Missouri wilderness as far west as the horizon. Our prospect was especially glorious when we arrived that first winter afternoon with the sun sinking swiftly behind the next range of hills. Above and to the south of us-- and thus out of sight from our porch--were the dining hall and conference building.

"Reminds me of the Open Place," I told her from the porch. She was in the doorway, inspecting the primitive furnishings.

The "Open Place" was where kids in my neighborhood used to hike, a clearing from which we could see famous Route 66 winding down the Fairfield plateau and across the Gasconade River valley. Bella had been bored often enough by the stories Billy Rhodes--my best friend growing up--and I used to tell about our adventures in those woods on the edge of town.

"You had a wonderful childhood," she admitted.

"You know, I think you're right. Of course, at the time I assumed all kids had the same good fortune. I really didn't know anything different."

"Well, many are just as happy as you were. But it's almost like the children in your neighborhood, the Circle, lived an especially enchanted life, something out of a fairy tale."

"Just like Nelson," I countered. "And then, all of a sudden, we grew up. *Ker-splat*, we ran smack into adulthood!"

"Well, let's don't dwell on that right now. I'm cold. Come on in and get the fire going."

While she began unpacking the food we'd brought with us, I carried wood in from the porch and followed the fire-building technique I'd learned in Boy Scouts years ago: several pages of newspaper rolled or wadded up; kindling stacked on next; three modest logs balanced on top. Such simple tasks are always satisfying, and I knew we'd soon have a roaring fire.

Billy and I had built more fires on our own out in our woods than we'd ever done with Boys Scouts. Sitting on the ground next to a campfire ringed with rocks from the Ozark hillside, we imagined many futures in which we were Texas cowboys, explorers of the African continent, soldiers like our dads. Ah, I never imagined the actual part I'd play in war.

There had been an official investigation of Operation Freeway. All those involved were

260

cleared of any potential charges. The one Vietnamese survivor admitted her relatives had been hiding in the forest, afraid to reveal themselves to unknown foreigners and such intimidating machinery.

As near as anyone could tell, this was yet one more exhausted family of refugees who had taken to the jungle hoping to avoid the very ambushes our project had been designed to eliminate. It was early in the morning, and they couldn't tell which way our plows were moving. Tragically, they stuck to their camouflaged hideout rather than attempt yet another flight from danger.

Three of us were working in a tight formation that day, and it was hard to know who brought what tree down on their little lean-to during our ferocious grinding up of the country. Our job was to make rubble in which no one could hide, in which no one could live. And we did.

Generally, guests at Mary's Peak were part of a larger body that met in corporate sessions. Church groups, company executives, academic departments discussed and presented in structured public venues and informal social gatherings.

We, however, were here on our own. We would, though, take meals in the dining hall next to state employees from the office of Dams and Hydroelectric Generator Maintenance. That group's weekend itinerary was posted on a bulletin board at the entrance. We were just winging it.

Well, I was winging it. In retrospect, it's clear that Bella had a precise itinerary.

I'm afraid I've always been a bit dense about other people's agendas. In childhood I wanted to see the world as an open book: what you see is what is out there. But grownups operate by a set of rules kept secret from children, and even best buddies have powerful desires they don't always acknowledge.

I've claimed that this naiveté is a Midwestern trait, perhaps a response fostered by the simple landscape pioneers confronted coming west over the Mississippi. We feel we should all be as direct and open as the prairie.

"Once we have the place warmed up," Bella said, "we can get started." She was in the kitchenette at the other end of the cabin's main room.

What exactly did she mean, "get started"? I'd agreed vaguely to talk about our marriage and things that were affecting it: my work, her work, the feud with Nelson, Jenny's choice of activities. (Of course, it had

262

occurred to me that this might be a chance to put some energy back in our sex life. Since Nelson's departure, it seemed neither of us was in the mood very often.)

"The fire's drawing perfectly," I called back to Bella. I wondered if she'd brought any special lingerie. The old uniform she'd worn at the Coral Court wouldn't work twice as a turn-on.

"Let's sit over here." She was pointing to the small dinette set beside a window. At each place she--or someone--had placed a yellow legal pad and a pencil.

"It's not quite lunch time. We could just watch the fire."

Some agendas are bigger than the individual's, of course. The forces of history determine the shape of the future, but its course become clear only when we can look behind us.

I remember being astounded to run into Billy on my second day in Vietnam. But two friends bumping into each other 10,000 miles from home wasn't really the remarkable coincidence I'd at first assumed. Many of the men in my generation were enlisting or being drafted. Our age and our education tagged us as likely for certain training and assignment. And many, many of those who were drafted came down on orders to use our new skills in the biggest military event of our time.

The channels in which Billy and I were destined to travel had been created by Lyndon Johnson, by the Cold War, by Richard Nixon, by post-colonial national identities emerging around the globe. We two Americans were carried along to the same destination by these national and international agendas. It wasn't accident or miracle or bizarre chance, but the product of a series of events now clearly visible in hindsight.

"Sit here," Bella said. "And let's each of us make a list of ten things we're afraid of."

XXXII.

I could see Bella was already well into the middle of her list. I wondered what fear would come second after staying married to me. If I put her leaving as what scared me the most, would she believe it? Or would she just conclude I was trying to use this retreat to pacify her, not really to make changes in myself or my life.

Through the window I saw a bird, probably a hawk, circling in the evening sun. He was lower than we were up in our hillside cabin. How free and easy his life seemed!

"Are we going to talk about all ten of our fears?" I asked.

"That's how the process works. A few are supposed to come to the top as our main worries, the things we each need help with."

So far I had two entries: Nelson and Mr. Banister. But I knew these did not represent insurmountable challenges. Nelson would come home or go his own way; the new route for the interstate would take the path I had proposed or another. I didn't think this psychological inquiry was going anywhere.

Bella got up from the table to make a cup of tea. Her sheet was filled, a page of indictments for my crimes, I assumed. I had added to my list of worries "career management," "understanding teenage girls," "accepting my bald spot," and "surviving root canal." I knew I'd have to put something from Vietnam down, but what and where?

"So, you ready?" Bella asked, setting her cup of tea on the table and straightening the pad before her.

"Ready as I'll ever be, I guess."

"All right. First, we read our lists, identifying one item at a time, taking turns. That way we not only get the range of each other's concerns, but we can determine their relative ranking."

"I see. Well, I've got Nelson on top. I think he needs to come home, realize this music business is a dead end, think more seriously about college. What worries you the most?"

I said it casually, but I was far from easy about what Bella would identify as her greatest fear. This moment of confrontation had come far more quickly in the weekend retreat than I'd anticipated. I felt cornered already.

"Jenny's body," Bella announced.

"Jenny's . . . ? What do you mean?"

"Oh, you men!" She leaned back in her chair and inspected me as a representative of that dense group. "You see the changes that affect your son, but you miss what's important in your daughter's future."

"How can you say that? I'm the one who's been insisting on her athletic potential, the opportunities in women's sports."

"What you're doing is pretending she's a boy, a physically gifted version of yourself who can devote her life to sports, a male obsession. You're dismissing all the old opportunities and obligations of women."

"The old opportunities? Aren't you pursuing new opportunities yourself, a career as counselor at Western? Don't you want Jenny to be, as feminists say, 'empowered'?"

"To be empowered is to be free to choose, old or genuinely new. Your version of the new is a man's version, restrained by what you can think of as something you'd want to do."

I hated this assertion that I was incapable of conceiving the options. How could I argue about things that were beyond my vision, impossible to picture?

I leaned back in my chair and studied Bella. "Okay," I said. "You, a mother, have a right to worry about Jenny. And you can probably see or feel or sense problems that escape me, a man, a father. But let me ask you something. Do you know what's really my greatest fear?"

When I asked that question, I assumed I alone knew the answer, that it was something Bella, a woman, a mother, would never be able to comprehend. How, then, did she know the awful truth?

"Mark," she said, "you're afraid you're living a lie."

"A lie? That's crazy!"

I said it with such anger, jerking back from the table, that Bella winced and looked down at her yellow pad. She wrapped both hands around her tea cup, as if she needed to warm them.

"I only say that," she went on softly, "because . . . because it's what I feel sometimes. That I'm hiding the truth."

"Oh, if you mean that we all keep secrets, I guess I can agree with you." I got up and went over to the refrigerator, thinking I could put ice in a glass and then a splash of Scotch. But I realized it was not even noon.

"Don't pull away, Mark. Remember, this is why we've come, to get things out in the open, to loosen the logjam." She turned in her chair to watch me, but she didn't get up.

"I'm . . . I'm just pouring a soda." I spilled Coke into my glass and returned to the table. "Let's go on to the second things on our list."

Turning to the fears we were willing to acknowledge defused the situation for the moment. As a further show of good faith, I went into far more detail about Banister's old Route 66 than was necessary. But when we broke for lunch, I knew all I had earned was a temporary delay. Bella was going to get back to what we each had been hiding from each other.

There was nothing startling about the rest of Bella's and my lists, unless you thought about what was absent. In the course of our lengthy afternoon session, she admitted to concerns about how the dean at Western viewed her work, about the chances that Nelson was experimenting with drugs, about unhappiness in my job after years of great satisfaction building roads and bridges. There was nothing written down about living with me.

I tried to make a lot out of my needing more regular exercise, as I knew Bella believed it would be therapeutic as well as healthful. I linked working out to a genuine fear I was becoming less attractive to her physically. Financial issues were a more obvious smokescreen, as we'd always been cautious in spending and investment.

Bella could tell I was trying to mix everything together into such a tangle that no single issue would come to the top. She would not back away, however, from the heart of the matter.

"Didn't Bill Pierce give you a book about Vietnam?" she asked at one point. "I think I saw you reading it. Maybe that's helping you find things that were never resolved for you?"

"It's a good book, a sad book. But I don't think it's showing me anything I didn't already know. So many of us didn't understand what we what were supposed to accomplish. Now, most people believe we had no business being there in the first place."

"How about once you got home? And when the war was over? Do you think those who served ever had closure?"

"Closure? No, I don't think we did."

"I didn't have closure on Vietnam either," Bella stated.

"But you weren't there. You didn't have to consider following orders, or challenging them. The confusion of the mission. How was the war traumatic for you?"

She had another cup of tea in front of her then. And again she looked into it, as if reading the past and not the future.

"Remember that demonstration my fellow graduate students and I ran into at Washington University?"

"Yeah. I guess." I didn't, in fact. But I recognized immediately that the associations her account was stirring up for me were decidedly unpleasant.

"Do you remember how I was singled out?"

"Singled out?"

"I didn't think you would. Well, anyway, someone said my 'boyfriend' was 'a cold-blooded killer.'"

"How did they know that?" Again, I jumped up from my chair. This time, I strode across the room to the fireplace and pushed the logs around violently with the poker.

Bella went on behind me, her voice very low. "The point was they couldn't know about you, about me, anything about us personally. But I was still hurt, so hurt. I didn't know how to respond, that day or later."

She sighed and sat up straighter. "Oh, the incident faded from my memory over time. Especially when you came back, we married, the family." She paused, and when she went on, her voice was shaky. "But now, all these years later, I find I'm haunted by that whole episode. Why couldn't I respond? Why did I let the lie begin?"

Seeing her struggle, my reserve melted, at least for the moment. "Oh, Bella, darling," I said. "What *is* it? I'm Okay. Don't you understand? I'm Okay now."

"You're OK?" she said, her eyes wide in disbelief. "You're OK? I don't believe it. And doesn't it matter that *I'm* not OK?"

XXXIII.

Bella got up from the table and went to the bathroom, weeping. Should I follow? No, I decided. She was crying, but not uncontrollably. I'll wait, give her time to compose herself. I can try to fix my list in the meantime, though this itemization of top fears now seems to be marching toward a dead end.

I remembered how trapped I'd always felt in the Army, where, required to follow orders, I had no options, no ways out. The feeling was perhaps at its worst when I returned to Vietnam from R & R in Australia. That five days' taste of freedom--and of Cindy from Sydney, of course!--made me realize how depressed I was that I could not control my own destiny.

Because of a paperwork mixup in the last stage of my return from R & R, I ended up stuck in Saigon for an extra day. I had no choice but to wait for transportation to the one place in all the world I didn't want to go.

With me that evening, by coincidence, was Warren Stevens, the itinerant Army reporter I'd gotten to know from his visits to our company. He was on his way out on a different story, and our paths had crossed late in the day at a MAC-V E-5 club.

Since I'd already been told I wouldn't be able to travel until morning, he had lingered with me, drinking beer and listening to a Filipino band play "Proud Mary" and other favorites of American boys far from home. We drank to dull our awareness of the fact that neither of us seemed to have any particular desire to go on.

Throughout the afternoon, Warren joked we could, if we wanted, catch "The Midnight Chopper," a helicopter mail run, which left Saigon nightly. As a reporter, he'd learned all sorts of ways to get around in-country, and he told me the route would take us at least close to my unit. "There's *always* The Midnight Chopper," he repeated cynically, asserting that the Army could get you where it wanted you to be whenever it wanted to.

Warren and I did leave the club around 9:00 in order to be on the grounds of Tan Son Nhut Air Base for the possible helicopter ride out. Unfortunately, that gave us time before midnight to emerge from the comfortable state of numbness we had attained at the club. In the shadows of a helicopter control tower, we came to a new awareness of ourselves as unhappy, reluctant soldiers.

Side by side on the ground, our legs stretched out before us, our backs up against a metal shed, we listened to a disembodied voice announce over a loudspeaker choppers coming and going. Each represented a potential ride for the dozen or so men trying to get to their destinations that night. But despite the fact that Tan Son Nhut was a center of travel north, south, east, and west, I felt cornered at the foot of the control tower.

We were enveloped in fog, mist, 100 per cent humidity, a palpable atmosphere of moisture. It clouded the night air so there was zero visibility. From unexpected, unpredictable directions, helicopters, their searchlights burning, suddenly took shape around us. Their pounding blades drowned out conversation.

Warren finally shouted that it was too late for us to travel that night, and I had to accept his conclusion . . . at first. The Midnight Chopper must have been scrubbed, and there would be no other ride going my way before daylight. Then, for no reason whatsoever, I felt we would escape into the night.

"Let's get a few hours sleep in a transients barracks," Warren proposed. "You can find ground transportation in the morning."

"But there is *always* a Midnight Chopper," I'd insisted peering up into the darkness. And just then, down through the fog came the sound of an arriving aircraft. Then, lights sliced through mist, and the gray-green belly of an Army helicopter descended toward earth. The infamous Midnight Chopper, it turned out, had just been running far behind schedule. (Well, there *was* a war going on!)

Still, eight soldiers, including Warren and me, were waiting for rides when that Huey descended, its motor whining, its blades thumping in the thick night air. And the two of us were the last of the eight in line.

Hueys had space--after their own crew, including pilot, copilot, and door-gunners-- for about six passengers. Even if this bird had been empty, there should not have been room for all those waiting.

That's what the flight control deck initially informed us over the loudspeaker, calling out that there was space for three riders. The first troops in line shouldered their gear and walked out to the chopper. The next two grunted and walked back toward the tower and the transients barracks somewhere beyond it.

That still left one person ahead of Warren and me, no seat for him, no possibility of a ride for us. Warren said, "Well, that's it. Let's give it up."

"No, wait."

Just when I was sure all places were full, the invisible controller, with no explanation, announced that there was room for one more. This guy seemed to have as many seats on the Midnight Chopper as he needed!

The man in front of us gave a jump, grabbed his stuff, and trotted out to get on board. That extra seat shouldn't have been there, and this surely should have been the end of the night for Warren and me.

"There it is," Warren said. "Now let's give it up, go get a few hours sleep--at least--before morning."

I caught his arm and said again, "Wait," because now my attention was focused on one of the door-gunners standing beside his ship. The outline of his figure is sharp before me still.

Helicopter crews wore one-piece, olive-drab flight suits and round, light-colored helmets. Each helmet had a thin microphone reaching around from the side, by the ear, to rest right in front of the mouth. The mikes almost touched the crew members' lips so that they could communicate while the noisy helicopter (and its weapons) operated.

I could see this gunner standing on the tarmac right beside the ship, electrical lines like umbilical cords still linking him to the chopper. But I could not see his face because the fog, the night, the distance made only an outline visible. The sphere of the helmet was clear, but the face in the middle was, from our vantage point, total darkness. I looked right at that darkness, that emptiness.

The last man ahead of us had gotten on board. The Midnight Chopper's engine continued to idle; the mist swirled; Warren pulled on my arm. I was still looking at my fellow soldier, the door-gunner, standing by his ship.

After perhaps thirty seconds of our staring at each other (or at least I believed my look was returned), the gunner started to walk toward us, continuing to gaze (I felt) directly at me.

He walked to the edge of the pad, right up to within two feet of us, and leaned forward. In the light from the tower above us his face suddenly appeared in the center of his helmet. It was the grinning, freckled face of a nineteen-year-old kid from, I now believe, a small town along Route 66. And he said with a happy smile, "You guys want a ride?"

Well, of course, we wanted a ride! That's what we had been waiting the past three hours for. But how did this boy have a seat for two more on a full bird? How did he know Warren and I were holding out beyond all reason for a place on this chopper?

To this day, I can't tell you the answer. I do know that Warren and I walked with our newfound, cheery friend across the tarmac. We got onto the helicopter, which somehow had two places in the canvas net seating right there by the door. We got on, buckled in, and were lifted right up into the night sky by this bosom buddy we had never seen before and never saw again.

Warren and I were lifted up into the sky, the Vietnamese night, as if by magic, extra passengers who were accommodated on an already full helicopter. The whole sequence of events has reminded me at times of Jesus' disciples on the road to Emmaus, puzzled by how many they were because they didn't recognize the risen Christ among their party.

And let me tell you something: a helicopter ride can be practically a spiritual experience, with the bird's vertical takeoff, its dip and sweep onto the horizontal. The side doors were open as usual (for the gunner at the ready), and I was right at the edge, loosely belted to the wall behind me. So I felt, for a moment, like an angel rising toward heaven.

Straight up and above the ground fog we flew. As the chopper swung to one side, turning north, I leaned out into the night air rushing past me. Saigon was spread out below me like some kingdom in a fairy tale. And now, the lights of that faraway city seemed to twinkle again in the fire of a Missouri cabin on the side of Mary's Peak.

XXXIV.

Always before, Warren's and my rising up into the sky had seemed an instance of unexpected, miraculous deliverance. But today, there was something different about that chopper ride, or at least about what I felt in it for the first time.

Instead of reliving once more the unearned escape, the ascent into the night sky, my mind traveled in the other direction, down to those lights blinking amid the fog on the streets of Saigon. Who was down there, I wondered? What were they doing in their tiny world represented by so many spots of light?

I heard the toilet flush, the bathroom door swing open. Bella came out wearing a brave smile.

"I feel so much better," she announced. Though her face was still red from crying-- and, I suspect, cold water splashed from the sink--she did have a genuine brightness.

I thumped my pad with the pencil's eraser and tried to look positive. "I've been fixing my list!" Didn't that sound like someone ready to resume the noble effort of confronting and resolving any troublesome matters between us?

"We're going to put your list away for a time." She sat back down at our little dinette set. "That's what we're going to do. We're going to talk about me for a change."

"For a change?" I did think this unfair, especially as she'd accused me so many times of not opening up. How could my refusal to relive the past keep her from talking about her problems? Still, I managed to deliver a smile with my objection.

"I've bottled this up so long," Bella continued, moving her tea cup and her legal pad off to the side of the table. "I almost didn't think I could get it out. This weekend I was just going to let you be the focus. You were going to tell me about . . . about the war, your nightmares, whatever difficult things that have blocked you off from the past."

At that moment, I still wasn't ready to dig up that last haunting image from Vietnam: Frank Middleton and the Rome Plow. Fortunately, Bella went on anyway.

"Now I think I need this talk, at least as much or maybe even more than you do." She took a deep breath. "Do you ever remember me talking about Sarah Johnson?"

282

"Sarah Johnson? No, I don't think so. At least that name doesn't ring a bell."

"Well, she was another graduate student at St. Louis in the psychology program. She was one of that group when those protesters attacked us at Washington University."

"Ah."

"Well, her brother was . . . um . . . I guess you'd call him a draft-dodger. He went to Canada."

"Um-hmm."

"At the time of that conference, Sarah hadn't seen . . . I don't remember his name. Anyway, she hadn't seen her brother in something like two years. He was, if I remember right, in Montreal, working construction. But what he'd wanted to be was a minister. She said he'd finished a year of college, then dropped out and became involved in the anti-war movement. He'd never filed as a conscientious objector, though, so when his draft notice arrived, he had to run away."

"Okay, I see. She thought I, who did serve, was a 'cold-blooded killer.'" Of course, I hoped she hadn't.

"She . . . she did. She thought anyone who let himself be drafted was . . . was either a coward or someone who was drawn to . . . to violence, to killing."

"And you let her say all those things about me?"

"Mark, at that time I hadn't seen you for, what? Ten months? You didn't write that much. I didn't know what you were doing."

"So you *did* believe it!" I was flabbergasted.

This was another reason I generally avoided discussions about Vietnam, the disapproval that automatically appeared on faces when others learned you were a veteran. Some people actually took a step backward whenever I confessed to having been in the Army, as if I might suddenly pull a grenade out of my pocket, slip the pin, and roll it at their feet. But I'd never suspected Bella felt that way about me.

Now she was tearing up again. I didn't have the strength or the wisdom or the love at that moment to comfort her. She was the counselor, I insisted to myself, who'd brought us to Mary's Peak.

Pulling a Kleenex from her pocket, she dabbed her eyes and went on. "Sarah responded to that protester who'd accosted me. She yelled back that our boys would never take up guns to fight in an unjust war. Her brother, she said, was working with international anti-war groups in Canada."

"I guess you couldn't very well say the same thing about me. But then again, we weren't officially engaged, as you remember. You had no obligation to defend me after you . . . after you said you wouldn't marry me"

"I'd said we should wait until you came back. A year was a long time. And we were so young."

"So, in that time you changed your mind about me?"

Bella rose and went to her purse on the sofa: more tissues. She was not really crying, but every few minutes she would gulp down a sob. And I could see tears well up in her eyes.

I was pretty much frozen in place at the table, an irrelevant list of ten top fears in front of me.

"Look," Bella went on, clutching a wad of kleenex. "Because we were the closest, Sarah and I had both turned to look at the protesters. I guess that was why one of them seemed to accuse me personally, because I was looking right at him. But when Sarah responded, she . . . she took my hand. She drew close as if we were the same, as if we both had men who'd done the same thing."

"Surely she knew that wasn't so?"

Now the tears came again. "I guess . . . I never . . . told her, or others . . . about you, about where you were exactly."

She had to go to the bathroom. I remained where I was.

The night panorama I'd scanned from the Midnight Chopper returned. And then I remembered viewing another city's lights not so many years ago--my own.

I have always admired St. Louis' Gateway Arch as an engineering marvel, a parabola-shaped, 630-foot high, stainless steel arch that straddles downtown on the Mississippi's river front. When Nelson was just an infant, Bella and I rode the tram system to the top one evening after dark. The arch hadn't been completed that long, so it was still quite a novelty. With our son in my arms, we looked west out over the city.

We were at a good point in our lives then. I had just obtained the job I'd always wanted, civil engineer for the Missouri Department of Transportation. Our marriage had been an extended honeymoon so far, perhaps because we'd first endured that year of separation while I was overseas. But we both also saw opportunities ahead in our professional lives.

Bella's graduate work had included an internship with a local hospital, which was then willing to hire her for part-time counseling on her own schedule. She had negotiated a baby-sitting swap with a couple of other young mothers in our neighborhood so that she could work three afternoons, as well as one evening a week (when I was at home).

Now, years later, where was I? Where were we?

I got up stiffly from the chair at the dinette table and walked over to the fire. The room was already warm, but I stirred the ashes anyway and piled three more logs on top.

As the fire licked at the new fuel, I recalled some of the engineering miracles behind the Gateway Arch, most of which are hidden from view. The concrete foundations, for instance, are sunk sixty feet into earth and thirty more feet into bedrock.

From the ground looking up, all you see is the sparkling stainless steel surface. If you slice one leg to produce a cross section, you'll find a perfect double-walled, equilateral triangle. The inside wall is carbon steel.

287

Reinforced concrete fills the space between inner and outer wall of each leg for the first 300 feet. But there's no real skeleton to the legs, just section added to section from ground to sky. Still, all the parts are so brilliantly united that, in a 150-mile per hour wind, the high point of the Arch will move only eighteen inches east or west, and not at all north-south.

Entering the tram, I was explaining these wonders of modern engineering to Bella. She joked that the arch should be a symbol of marriage. We were each an anchored leg, she said, together an unshakable perfect shape.

When Bella emerged from her second session in the bathroom, I must have felt that some unearthly wind had blown through our union, a wind no manmade structure could withstand. My voice cracked as I asked her, "Have you . . . have you been ashamed of me all these years?"

XXXV.

Bella stopped in the middle of the room, staring at me. "Ashamed of you? No. Hasn't it occurred to you that I should be ashamed of myself?"

Again, I was puzzled. She hadn't been to war, hadn't had to do or not do anything. Why would she be ashamed or not ashamed? She was part of the home front, waiting for people like me--well, for me specifically--to come home.

I was the one, of course, with the guilty conscience, even if I'd done a pretty good job of hiding it for more than a decade. "Maybe," I suggested. "Maybe you should explain things to me. Maybe it *is* your time to talk and mine to listen." Maybe I was once again being careful to avoid having to explain my own shame.

"All right," she agreed. "Let's put away both lists. We can sit in front of the fire . . . if we don't burn up!"

My fire was positively roaring now, and she laughed at the sight. "Come on, slide the sofa back. It's too close. Can you spread the logs out a bit, so it burns with a little less heat?"

I was grateful to be given simple tasks to perform. Our retreat had already been far harder (and hotter!) than I'd foreseen. Later, I'd come to understand that, despite her tears, Bella was controlling the stages and the direction of this extended counseling session pretty much as she'd planned.

"So," she said, once we were settled on the sofa. "So, let me tell you one more thing about that year you were gone. Wait, I have to get something for you. It's in my bag."

I looked at the fire, less intense now, but still sending sparks snapping up the chimney. Could I last another day of this soul-searching? We were supposed to leave by mid-afternoon tomorrow in order to be home for dinner with Jenny. Not, of course, with Nelson, the disaffected son. If I could get by this Wash U. thing with Bella, maybe I could hold on until it was time to pack up and come down from the mountain.

Bella slipped beside me onto the sofa, a plastic shopping back on her lap, and began her tale.

"At St. Louis that year, I was far from home, really for the first time. Sure, I'd gone away to my undergraduate college, but at such a traditional Southern women's school it was more like an extension of home. I had housemothers and fatherly professors and 400 sisters, so I was never lonely. My parents could come get me for a weekend or holiday anytime I wanted."

"I see. And you've told me how the Midwest wasn't a very friendly place for you at first."

"That's right. I didn't know the people or how things are done out here. And graduate school was intimidating. I felt that we were all in competition or something. So, my reaction was to withdraw, curl up like a threatened animal into my protective shell, and study, study, study."

"I guess I was thinking of other things at the time."

"Sure, sure. You had to." We were shoulder to shoulder on the sofa, but she now she took my hand in hers. "I threw myself into my work that year, especially the first term. If I wasn't in the lab or the library, I was up late in the graduate dorm."

I noticed that the fire had settled down to an even glow, warming us nicely at this distance.

"Surely you had some fun?"

"You're right. That happened when I decided to launch a new project, something that was unrelated to studying but that did give me pleasure. My mother had always wanted me to take it up."

"And that was?"

"Knitting."

Ah, now Jenny's recent interest in embroidery made a bit more sense. Her mother was behind it for some reason, a reason no mere man could fathom. Bella had, so far as I'd known, never done much in that line since, especially while the children were young and kept us both busy.

"I don't see how knitting solved the problem of your loneliness."

"It didn't completely, but it still helped in a way. You see, my Mom taught me long-distance. She wrote two letters a week, and with each letter--in addition to news from home--she sent me instructions on what to do next."

"So, besides courses in psychology, you were taking one in sweater making."

"That's right, though it wasn't so much sweaters at first as socks and mittens."

The picture I had of Bella in all this wasn't attractive: shivering in her dorm room, books open on the desk, and the bed covered with balls of yarn, pairs of knitting needles, pages of instruction.

"It was cold that year here in St. Louis?" I asked.

"Well, yes, but that's not the reason for knitting winter things. That went back to the war. Not your war, Daddy's war."

"Oh, yes. Knitting for World War II GI's, who were slogging around Europe in the winters of . . . what would it have been--1943, 1944?"

"That's right. But you see the problem, don't you, with my knitting?"

"Uh, no. I mean, it was something to do, right? A break from study. And you were connecting with your mother. You probably called from time to time to go over hard parts--casting off, or whatever it's called."

"I did call, but . . . " She took a deep, shaky breath. I feared she was going to start crying hard again. "But there wasn't the same purpose, you see. Not like when she and her friends where shipping boxes of knitted goods to men overseas."

"Well, yes. I don't recall getting anything in the mail."

"That's right. The nation was united in that earlier war, which wasn't the case with Vietnam. Plus, you were in the jungle, Mark, the tropics. The last thing you needed was mittens." Now she did shudder, a sigh becoming a sob.

"You mean you really wanted them to be for me?"

"I knitted sweaters for you, Mark. And afghans and hats, and then vests and gloves and ear muff covers. The saddest were the bandages. I filled boxes and boxes. Boxes, all for you."

"But I never got them. I've never even seen them!"

"I couldn't send them. It was too confusing. When you came back, when I saw you, you didn't want to talk about what you'd seen, what you did. You were ready to get married and get on with what you'd dreamed about the whole time, being an engineer."

"I have to admit you're right there."

"So, I . . . I kept them until the day before our wedding. Then, I asked my Mom to donate them to the Salvation Army or someone while we were on our honeymoon. All but one piece."

The bag rustled and she lay across my knee a beautiful red, white, and blue scarf. It was fine wool, skillfully done.

"I never gave it to you, Mark. I'm not sure why. But I just happened to be carrying it in my bag that day Sarah Johnson assured the anti-war protesters that we, too, despised all those cold-blooded killers."

I took a deep breath. "I guess it's time for me to show you what I've got hidden in my bag." I started to get up.

"All right, but in just a minute. I know now why I couldn't give this to you, and why I couldn't separate myself from Sarah Johnson, who was very much against the war: I never felt I knew enough to take a stand in those days, at least in public."

"You mean you weren't going either to rallies supporting the troops or to anti-war protests?"

"That's right. I'd retreated to a narrow world, where I could ignore these difficult issues. You see, despite being a college graduate, I still felt so . . . well, so young." She seemed puzzled still, either at her former indecisiveness or at the dilemma she'd faced then.

"But you've been a regular political activist for years. You're a registered Democrat, you were one of the first to join the M.A.D.D. crusade, you give money regularly to a dozen charities through church."

"That's now, not then. I guess I finally grew up, maybe when Nelson was born. Or at least I decided I couldn't wait forever."

"Hmm. Maybe I've done the same thing, concentrated on building bridges and roads, ignoring politics."

Bella got up from the sofa and stood closer to the fire, as if now she'd gotten cold.

"I've always felt awful for not standing up for you that day, for letting Sarah Johnson claim me. I'm sorry."

I stood up too and put my arms around her. "You shouldn't feel bad, for heaven's sake. I never knew. I mean I just assumed you didn't . . . that you didn't despise me. Besides, I have more to apologize for. Let me show you something."

I went into the bedroom and returned carrying my Bronze Star.

XXXVI.

This clearly was the opportunity to tell Bella about the Vietnamese family hiding in the jungle, the family buried by the U.S. of A. one terrible day in a war that, we now know, had lost its focus and its purpose. But I didn't repeat then what I'd explained earlier to Bill. Surprising myself, I instead unearthed Frank Middleton's story.

Oh, I did explain in more detail than I'd ever given her before the nature of the work combat engineers did in Vietnam, the clearing and the different kinds of construction. And Bella probably understood that, when I also talked about destruction, I meant we did damage to more than vegetation. She was kind enough not to demand any more of the specifics than I was providing. She could see I was struggling.

"Every day must have been hard," she admitted.

"Hard at first because it was all so new, all scary. Then, it became incredibly boring and repetitive. And toward the end, you began to worry that you wouldn't get out, some last minute bit of bad luck."

"You were being just as deceptive as I was, though. You wrote cheerful letters, telling me you were just fine, always working in safe areas."

"That probably was true, more true than I knew myself until I'd been home for a while. Lots of times we worked with the local population on the friendliest of terms. It's just that we were never sure. Were they the good guys, or the bad guys?"

As trying as it was, of course, most of the men I worked with knew they still had a far better assignment than the grunts who were ordered to "search and destroy" the enemy. Many of them genuinely hoped for the "million dollar wound"--an injury from which you would recover fully, but only after such a long time of convalescence that you would not be returned to combat.

Those way in the rear, facing at most rare and random danger, hoped simply to last out their tours. And those somewhere in between, like us engineers, often became complacent. We had to summon patience where grunts required courage.

"Tell me about this, then." Bella held up the medal, which, while packing, I'd taken from its hiding place in the back of a desk drawer. I don't think I'd looked at it twice since I'd come home. Bella had snapped open the black case it came in, showing the star, ribbon, and bar resting on gold lining. "It's yours?"

"It is. I was awarded the Bronze Star at the end of my tour, for what they call 'meritorious service,' not valor. Believe me, I'm not guilty of genuine heroism in the line of fire or anything like that."

"I should be proud of you, though, shouldn't I? Even if the war ended badly, you did your duty well."

"I wish I knew how you're supposed to feel. I still don't know how I feel, for that matter." I paused and studied the fire again. "Do we need to add a log?"

"Not yet. Maybe stir it up some; make sure it's getting air." When I'd done that and sat back down, she leaned into me, shoulder against shoulder.

I gestured toward the bedroom. "I was thinking earlier, when you were . . . in there. I was thinking about the St. Louis Arch, the Gateway Arch."

"All right." From her uncertain tone, I realized this had come as an unexpected change of subject. I went on anyway, hoping I could get where I wanted to be somehow with this history.

"It's what you call a 'catenary curve,' an inverted form of what you'd see if you hung a rope between two spots. When you look from the ground, of course, it's a catenary curve upside down. Remember going up that first time?"

"When Nelson was a baby. Yes, of course, I do. It's pretty spectacular. There are no hills nearby, and of course the Illinois side is completely flat, so you can see forever."

"Well, there are some bluffs over there, where the river has eaten away and left rock walls. But, up in the Arch, they seem small. You feel above it all, especially at night."

The cabin fire, its sparks rising, recalled the lights of Saigon as seen from the Midnight Chopper. I went on with my story, determined now, surprisingly, to get it all out at last.

We had been working in one area for over a week, another of those operations to clear roadside jungle and eliminate the possibility of ambush against supply convoys and local traffic. We were told no Viet Cong had been anywhere close since a major campaign by ARVN troops a year earlier. Our

300

mission was to prevent any return of enemy forces to the region.

We cut trees and bushes on each side of the road, working in three-plow teams to bring anything standing down to the ground. Armored personnel carriers stayed on the high roadbed, and infantry patrols moved in and out of the jungle to provide security. In mostly flat land, the major problem we faced was bogging down in swamp or marsh.

As often happens, though, security got lax over time. Many of the grunts were shorttimers, rotating out of the bush for their last weeks. They viewed this assignment as easy duty, convincing themselves that the kind of alertness they'd had to maintain elsewhere wasn't necessary here.

The engineers, too, let up, thinking primarily about how many more acres needed to be cleared, whether the machines required repair, how close we were to our next standdown. We didn't anticipate attack or accident.

"Poor Frank Middleton," I told Bella. "In the wrong place at the wrong time. And he was even keeping his pot and his driving separate."

I had a sharp image of Frank getting down from his plow in the middle of a long afternoon, sweat pouring off his face, his fatigues soaked. He is smiling, pleased with himself and believing in a certain camaraderie with the other drivers. He is slipping behind a big tree to relieve himself.

"You don't have to tell me everything," she said. "But he was killed? In an attack?"

"That's the saddest part. Not rockets or mortars or any weapon. He was . . . well, he was kind of 'road kill'."

The smiling Frank in my memory steps out from behind the tree, ready to mow more forest. I am just turning around to see if he's done at the instant he's hit.

Like the rest of us, Middleton had had to drive many days in a row, so his system was temporarily cleansed of the worst stuff he'd ingested. He'd had only a couple of beers the night before, too exhausted to stay up and drink. Right then he was wide awake.

I've often wondered what his life would have been like if he'd survived. Nothing he ever said about his Oklahoma working class background suggested he'd do more than follow his father as metalworker in a winch-manufacturing plant. But what drove him to drugs in Vietnam may have blocked even that modest ambition.

302

"Since we worked in teams, I'd stopped my plow, too, perhaps twenty yards in front of Frank. Peter Ward was idling behind him, or at least that's what I thought. He should have been. And maybe he was, but obviously he was moving again at the instant of Frank's death.

"I heard the sound of Ward's machine, but for some reason I thought it was one of the APCs rumbling off road to check something out. Anyway, at the very moment I turned and saw Frank step out from behind the tree, ready to get back in harness, the giant blade of Ward's plow hit him. Total accident. He hadn't seen him go behind the tree."

Bella stiffened, I could hear her sharp intake of breath.

I had to gather myself to go on. "It's a lesson in basic physics: two-ton clearing blade hits 140-pound man. Ward was swinging the oversized blade in a routine maneuver, getting ready to drive the reinforced steel 'stinger' on one end into a huge trunk, twisting the tractor at the same time. Instantaneous."

I don't give any more detail: how practically every bone in

Frank's body and skull is fractured; how the satisfied smile of a man who's just emptied his bladder never leaves his face; how Frank remains perfectly upright flying across space, a vertical man-doll walking in air away from Ward's machine; how he smacks directly into my own plow.

Still holding my hand, Bella says nothing. Tears are in my eyes, but I don't want to cry. She lets me alone, except for the steady pressure of her hand, until my breathing evens out.

And then she asks, "Mark, why did you get the Bronze Star?"

"It's crazy really," I say, swallowing, just as she had earlier, what could have been a sob. "The C.O. liked how I handled the Rome Plow." A wild laugh escapes me. "Not that I was an especially good soldier, or remembered the mission, or anything like that. It's a civilian skill I had, and still have, I guess. Honey, I got a medal for being a good driver!"

XXXVII

I wasn't back in the saddle again, but back in the endodontist's chair, mouth wide open and wondering if this root canal process would ever be over.

Dr. Hartman, however, announced cheerily, "Everything looks good here. We just need to do a little shaping. Then, we'll make an impression."

Of course, this wasn't my final visit to her office. After the hollowing out of that first day, she had packed the tooth with some kind of gunk to prevent infection and to let all the tissues calm down. She put a temporary cap on the tooth; but that would be replaced first (today) with a temporary crown, then (in a few weeks) with a permanent one.

With my feet once more higher than my head and a whining, high-speed drill aimed at my mouth, it was another time for marching--that is, mindlessly going from one moment to the next. It's one of the few military notions I've adopted, keeping in step with a commander or a power greater than the individual.

"I saw your wife last week," Dr. Hartman observed as she worked.

I could only raise my eyebrows in a question, of course, not speak. (In this unpleasant, heels-over-head position, perhaps I'm *lowering* my eyebrows?) She was smearing a jelly-like substance over the tooth and its neighbors. I could have said, "*Ahg, nuhg, ahg*?" of course, but I chose to communicate by gesture alone.

"At the Mothers Against Drunk Driving meeting."

I produced an "*Ah*" that had only a modest gurgle to it.

"We talked for some time, not just about your tooth."

I hoped my mouth had an agreeable smile on it, but I couldn't tell. Dr. Hartman tested the jelly to see if it was hardening in the appropriate manner. It would produce the impression that some dental technician would then turn into a plaster model. And from that, the technician--or some computer-- would generate a new tooth--the better to bite you with, my dear. Hmm--perhaps they could make a whole new me!

"I don't know what you've been doing lately," she said, "but it must be the right thing. Bella praised you as the best husband any woman could ever have."

Now I really went for some version of a smile. And my little heart went "*Ahg, nuhg, ahg!*" I imagined myself saying that Bella was better than the best wife any man could have.

We had driven back from Mary's Peak renewed. Not that we'd been spared tears over the weekend. Nor am I sure hers exceeded mine. But the dam had broken in some ways for both of us.

Bella seemed to know that the worst was over for her, a barrier crossed. The best news for me was her announcement that she wouldn't be using the efficiency apartment at Western after all. I promised to work harder at deserving that concession.

Vietnam memories that had haunted me for years, jogged into action months ago by Tony Roberts' audio tape and the visit of two Phyllises, were now at least out in the open. But I did worry that still more adjustment would be required over time. All I'd figured out so far was that I wanted to talk to Bill Pierce again.

From our perch on Mary's Peak, Bella and I had driven down to the valley through a fresh falling snow. Fortunately, this storm was just coming in from the west, and the roads we would take north and east were not covered. These big wet flakes would pile up on branches and fence posts and the tops of bushes, but not pavement. It was beautiful, but not threatening.

"Now I just need to put this temporary crown on, and you're set to go," Dr. Hartman explained. Stay away from extreme hot or cold for a few hours, of course. And no peanut brittle until the tooth is completely done!"

I was pleased: a quite painless procedure. Dr. Hartman promised that the installation of the permanent crown would be equally uneventful. It would be great to chew again without anxiety. Except for continuing concerns about Nelson, I realized, I might be in for a quieter time now, at least at home.

In the mail that Jenny had stacked on the kitchen table, however, was a letter from Ralph Banister that required an answer. He was offering me, in a sense, a job.

In league with a group of businessmen, local politicians, and conservationists, he had established the First Organization of Route 66 Missourians, or F.O.R.M. Their goals were to promote preservation of the old highway, restoration of landmark buildings along its corridor, and collection of material related to Route 66 and its history.

Ralph claimed that this group had nearly completed a deal with the governor and national transportation agencies concerning his land and the stretch of old road that ran through it. But F.O.R.M. needed a volunteer to provide expertise in the formalization and implementation of this scheme. They needed, that is, an engineer. And Banister wanted me to accept the post.

Crazy at it sounds, I didn't reject the idea immediately. True, I'd spent the last few years planning for a new stretch of interstate that would take away Banister's farm and the pavement he'd preserved. Now I was considering joining the effort to save the old road and abandon what all my engineering training told me was the correct path for the new highway.

As the debate about the plan had become more involved and more tiresome, I'd lost some of my original energy for the project. The struggle to come to terms with my own past had taken center stage instead. If I'd achieved a genuine breakthrough on that front at Mary's Peak, perhaps I'd now have time for extra projects, even volunteer activities like historic preservation.

I was also learning that my children didn't seem to need my attention quite so much as I'd thought. Nelson was coming by every few days to pick up things he needed (and do his laundry), but he communicated mostly with Bella. Jenny was settling into a routine in which her spare time was spent playing soccer, visiting with friends, or embroidering that country village scene.

Bella's work was time-consuming, though she'd proposed more retreats for the two of us--not as therapy, but as pure recreation. She even promised to bring new lingerie from Victoria's Secret on a return to the Coral Court, if I would take her dancing first.

In the end, I agreed to meet Ralph one more time at the Diamonds and hear him out. And so, just a few days before I was scheduled to get the permanent crown on my rebuilt tooth, I was once again driving out Interstate 44, down the route of old Route 66. Miraculously, the Sunset Hills exchange with I-270 had reached a new, more comfortable stage in which westbound traffic moved smoothly down to and across the Meramec River.

On a sudden whim, I left the interstate at Eureka, wondering what it would be like to follow more closely the actual path of what Ralph often called "America's Main Street."

St. Louis' Manchester Road had become a state highway out here, and it lay on the Route 66 of early days, the 1920s and 1930s.

I was running ahead of schedule (having anticipated delay at the old bottleneck) and encountered little traffic (some of that "farm use") all the way to Gray Summit. It gave me time to think over once more the conclusions I'd reached with Bella.

Despite the sense of relief coming from our retreat at Mary's Peak, I had realized something else still needed to be done. I had to take an action of some kind or make some statement to bring lasting resolution to this struggle. I wanted reconciliation with myself, I guess, with the man who'd served his country but then wanted to forget that he had.

Bella told me, "I think my activism-- M.A.D.D, the P.T.A., local politics--countered the regret I felt for indecision at the time of Vietnam. I'm glad I told you about Sarah and that confrontation, but I didn't need to do it."

"But you think I have to do more than get the whole story out to you?"

"Maybe. I mean, it's up to you. But . . . well, you've been honest with yourself and with me. But it might be that you have to be more comfortable as a veteran in your public life."

"You mean, start attending V.F.W. meetings?" I'd never been much of a joiner. It's another Midwestern thing Bella has never fully accepted: you're supposed to do everything on your own, the self-reliance of my father and his Swedish immigrant father.

"That may not be right for you. You should talk with Nelson, for one thing."

"And with Jenny," I added, recalling the dream I'd had where she appeared as a bloodied soldier.

"With Jenny--yes. That's a good idea. She will be glad you want to."

"But what else?" I wondered.

Pulling into the Diamonds' parking lot a few weeks later, I knew, all of a sudden, exactly what I should do.

XXXVIII

"Let's take a table over there in the corner," Ralph suggested. It gave us views east and south through plate glass windows. "Hi, Linda. How are you today?"

Linda was the waitress, a slim woman close to my age. The warm smile with which she responded to Ralph suggested he was a regular.

You could go through a cafeteria line at the Diamonds or get table service. I was letting Banister decide how to proceed. If he was going to try to make the idea of reversing highway department policy palatable, I figured he needed every advantage. How could I have known how once again he cleverly had foreseen where our conversation would end?

"Let me tell you a story while we wait for our food," he suggested. I was scanning the view outside the restaurant, cars parked in front and then, on the interstate below us, steady, fast-moving traffic. I also listened to Ralph's account of his adolescent crush on one Carolyn Summit

"She was about the prettiest thing I'd ever seen that first year of my high school.

Goodness, when would that have been? Probably right in the middle of the Roaring Twenties."

The Diamonds, "World's Largest Roadside Restaurant," had been built in 1927 and was therefore as old as "The Mother Road. After a fire it was rebuilt in 1948. The owners moved the establishment in the mid-1960s when a highway rerouting left them out of sight of travelers. They had originally been right at the center of traffic coming together from U.S. highways 50 and 66.

"Ah, but it seems like yesterday," Ralph went on. "You know how that works, don't you?"

Linda came with my coffee and his tea.

"Well, anyway, I wasn't the only one who worshipped Carolyn from afar--from afar quite literally!" He chuckled. "There was a crowd of us boys in Pacific gawking at her flapper hairdo, her cute little figure, those slim dresses. She had a reputation!"

"I know the kind of girl you mean," I said, thinking of Cathy Williams, the neighborhood beauty when I was growing up. A town celebrity, she later went from starring in college musicals to becoming, for a few years, a Hollywood actress.

"Everyone in my set was crazy about Carolyn, even though we knew she was just amusing herself with us. She was a flirt, but you might also say she taught us how to fall in love."

I understood the type. I had been too reserved at that age to play romantic games. My childhood crush on Marcia Terrell was indulged because I was sure she liked me. Someone with more self-confidence, like Susan Bell, made me withdraw and play safe.

"Carolyn had started this little game with us boys. Whoever could climb Wilson's Point earned the right to kiss her. She would wait at the top, the goal of our fantasies."

"How did she get up there herself?" I assumed Ralph was talking about a limestone bluff, common in these counties. Especially along the Meramec, they rise up hundreds of feet. Climbing is difficult and even dangerous because the rock is soft and crumbly.

"Well now, that was a bit of a mystery. We all had to stay in a group by this fence gate. Carolyn would go through the gate, cross a little clearing, and then disappear into the woods. About ten minutes later, we could see her up on the Point, waving down to us. And then we could start off one by one to try to earn the prize, one kiss from this little charmer."

"So, she went up the way you were supposed to?"

"She had tied bits of red ribbon to mark the exact climbing route. Sam Batteen always followed her first. He was kind of her beau then, I guess. Although only a year older than me, he was very popular, starting center for our basketball team as a sophomore. I can still see him waving to the rest of us, then bending down to kiss Carolyn right on the lips."

Linda brought our food, and there was a gap in conversation while we arranged the table, salted the vegetables, declined the ketchup. I wondered if tumbling pigeons were about to make an appearance on Wilson's Point, perhaps spinning and twirling from Carolyn down to the drooling boys at the fence gate.

"Oh, I need to show you this," Ralph said. He pulled a thick envelope out of his suit jacket pocket. "Take a look."

Rather than a bunch of sheets, it was a single large piece of paper folded over on itself. I had to push back from the table a bit and turn in my chair to spread out and view the whole thing.

"This is the plan we've got preliminary approval on. We're just dotting the *t*'s and crossing the *i*'s." I could tell from his grin that the mixing of letters was intentional. "But, once you look it over, I can explain what I'd like you to do."

I took a bite of sandwich, then a drink of coffee, then a view of the diagram. It showed the Banister land with the old stretch of Route 66 pavement at the center. A new path for the four-lane interstate was cleanly drawn. I knew when I saw it that it was an ingenious solution to the problem.

"Who did this?" I asked, because it was quite professional. And I was pretty sure no one in my department had drafted it.

"Oh, my son-in-law--the one down in Tulsa--he's an engineer. He did this for me."

"Why didn't you ask him to be the consulting engineer."

"Well . . . for one thing, you're a lot closer to the site."

His hesitation made me ask, "And . . . ?"

His second answer was typically enigmatic. "Mark, it's the right job for the right man."

The right man for the job? What did that mean? Yes, I could build roads. And my backing of this design, as the original project engineer, would probably erase any remaining opposition.

Maybe Ralph meant something else as well: that it was the right job for me. Did this old-timer know I needed to admit that building never occurs in a vacuum? Whether it's roads and bridges in Southeast Asia or interstate highways in the heartland of America, to build one thing almost always means to tear down another. What Ralph was offering might have been a special case: constructing for the future while preserving the past.

I realized that I would be lucky to find just this kind of project at just this moment in my life, a time when I was finally acknowledging a long-hidden piece of my own history. On Mary's Peak I'd learned that my year in Vietnam had changed who I'd been and what I later became. Now I had to preserve that uncovered piece of myself in order to build a future I could believe in. The Route 66 project might be a key element of my own healing.

What Banister's son-in-law had envisioned was a split highway, the east-moving two lanes running around the mountain to the north of the farm and the west lanes passing across the same land but narrowly avoiding the old pavement. The entire property was to be devoted to the idea of America's vision of itself as a land of opportunity. It exists today, in fact, as Route 66 National Gateway Park, a center that hosts hundreds of thousands of visitors to its museum (Ralph and Sarah's old house, of course, neatly remodeled).

I asked Ralph, "How did that girl-- Carolyn, was it?--how did she get to the top of the bluff?:"

"Oh, that! Well, there were two tricks involved there. The first I figured out the following year, when I was older."

"We do get wiser as we age, I hope."

"I don't know if I was that much smarter, but I was bigger. I'd had a growth spurt between ninth and tenth grade, and that made a big difference in getting to the top of Wilson's Point."

"How so?"

"Remember how I told you Batteen was tall, one of our best basketball players? Well, it's size that did it. You needed a certain inseam length and wing span to reach extra unmarked toe and hand holds going up the cliff. Tom was the first of our age group to make it. I simply couldn't get from one ribbon-marked point to the next without another year's height. Eventually, I realized all the guys who couldn't earn a kiss were shorties."

"But Carolyn could do it? She must have been larger than I imagined."

"Oh, no. She never climbed the bluff at all. Sam had put the flags up there for her. It was their little joke on all us runts. What she did was easy: go around the cliff and walk up a gentle slope on the back side."

"So you never saw her come from behind the hill?"

"I think Sam must have distracted us. We would later watch him rise up--head, shoulders, back. But the first we ever saw of Carolyn, she was waving and smiling down at us."

I saw myself at that fence gate looking up. When (after having talked it all over with Bella) I told Ralph I'd take the volunteer position of engineering consultant, I felt I would have deserved Carolyn's kiss at least.

XXXIX.

One Sunday, not long after the retreat at Mary's Peak and my meeting with Ralph, I had the talk with Bill Pierce I had wanted. We were sitting on a bench outside of church, along the sidewalk that skirted a small plot of lawn and then wound through a stand of trees to the rectory. Our wives were at a prolonged, after-church meeting of the Episcopal Church Women.

This was one of those unexpected, midwinter spring days. The temperature had shot up to 60 degrees, the sun was bright, and the earth pretended it would burst forth tomorrow in greenery. Snow would arrive by Monday night, of course, reminding us, like the groundhog who had recently seen his shadow, that genuine blossoming was weeks away. But right now, it's great to be alive.

Bill made a confession. "In some ways, I'd be happier if I could say I'd survived actual combat, if I'd seen things too horrible to talk about. People would be sympathetic, no matter what they thought about the war--and they wouldn't ask questions."

"I know what you mean. Even if they don't say it, it's always a question at the front of their minds: 'Did you kill someone?' 'Did you watch someone die?'"

"Right. When you don't answer, they assume you did, which isn't true in my case. At least, I didn't see anyone die in battle."

"The same goes for me."

"It's true that I don't particularly want to talk about what I saw in the hospital when I was called in to help, the mutilated faces, the guys who couldn't talk, couldn't see."

I recalled the Vietnamese family torn up by our plows, the one woman who survived. Hardly the hero that or any other day, I'd stood back to let the medics take care of the mess. It was the same on the day Frank was flattened.

Bill went on. "People say doctors and dentists face that all the time in their jobs. So what's the big deal? 'War is hell,' they think. 'Why don't you just go on with the business of living? What do you want? A giant thank you?'"

I recall that, while all my family and friends were glad I came home safely, only my older brother, Charles, made a deliberate effort to say he appreciated what I'd done.

"It wasn't like other wars, or at least modern American wars. We couldn't feel proud of what we did, but we didn't want to confess to guilt either. People didn't know what to say to us."

"Most of us have had to make a private peace with ourselves."

I recalled that Bill's first marriage had been a casualty of the war, probably before he made that separate peace. "Were you listening to John's sermon this morning? I know I don't always."

Bill gave a short laugh. "I'm usually good for the main points. Moses on the mountaintop, I got that much."

"Yeah. John linked it to Martin Luther King. I guess we're not much past his birthday, the new national holiday. King said he'd been to 'the mountaintop'--when was it? The day he died?"

"The day before. He was in Memphis supporting striking sanitation workers there. But he talked about having come close to death in an earlier incident. Now he could see the Promised Land."

"And he wasn't afraid of death, his death. He had a greater vision. I guess that's what I've been waiting for--a sense that I've come to the mountaintop. Not that all struggles are over, and certainly not that I'm Moses or Martin Luther King!"

"King protested the war, too, of course. He thought blacks were doing more than their share of the dying."

I knew that a lot of whites took advantage of college deferments as long as they lasted. And anyone who was well off or well connected had more ways to seek medical exemptions and safe posts in the National Guard. Oddly, it no longer bothered me that I'd been drafted, even though I recognized some injustice in the system. My current job was to accept responsibility for what I had done, as well as what I hadn't done. Surprisingly, I was finding myself close to that goal.

What had given me the strength to finish my marching time in Vietnam? Perhaps that was the final question I had to ask myself. And once more, my enigmatic new associate, Ralph Banister, seemed to be helping me see the answer.

His whole idea about Route 66 was starting to make more sense to me: it was a road of dreams. Having read more of the material he'd provided me for the engineer's post, I'd learned that those who first proposed a connected highway running from

Chicago to California saw it as something to link East and West. The idea had endorsed growth and opportunity, America's very identity.

Growing up in a little town along this famous highway, I had no daily thoughts about Okies fleeing the dust bowl in the Depression for a better life further west. Nor were those World War II GI's Ralph had told me about--who followed the same path by train to West Coast bases and the Pacific Theater--regular topics of conversation in the Circle. Still, such figures and their associations with Route 66 were embedded in the culture that enveloped me as I came of age.

Americans have forever fled bad times to make fresh starts in the territories. This started with the Pilgrims coming to the New World. From what we neighborhood kids called the Open Place, we could always see the Mother Road snaking around Ozark hills and across Missouri's rivers toward an enchanted, imagined future.

How did one get to such a goal, the fulfillment of dreams? Well, the same way, I suppose, that I had delivered the *Fairfield Daily Mirror* to stores and residences when I was in junior high school; the same way I had hauled and sorted books at Martin's Tire's,

325

unlikely paperback and magazine distributor for Phipps County; the same way I'd mopped the floor at the downtown Rexall's when I was in high school--one step at a time, putting one foot in front of the other, marching.

My grandfather, who crossed the Atlantic from Scandinavia, and my father, who had seen service in Africa and Italy, had established a pattern I subconsciously followed. They had made their marches.

In the days I had known her, my grandmother stayed close to the little church she'd helped found. My mother stood in the kitchen of our little house on Limestone Drive to nurture a growing family. But both of them also took on the next chore every day in an extended succession of tasks and responsibilities.

So, when I fired up the Rome Plow in one place after another in South Vietnam, I was aided by an ancestry of achievement, by a heritage of resolve--ghosts, if you will, but ghosts of great vitality. Sadly, significant groups of Americans have sometimes been cut off from that vitality.

I remembered poor Frank Middleton again, not, this time, his painfully ironic death, what I still think of as a traffic accident.

But I recalled how Frank in his ignorance failed to tap into the American Dream even when he'd been in contact with it.

Warren Stevens had been on another of his visits to our company during a standdown. Most of us were drinking beer that night, but Frank had gotten into some good stuff and was running off at the mouth.

"I been to St. Louie once," he told me, asserting a friendship when all we really shared was our being plow drivers. "Went to that there Arch downtown. Damnedest thing I ever saw!"

"The Gateway Arch," Stevens said. "Gateway to the West, all that territory Jefferson bought from the French that really belonged to Native Americans in the first place."

"Damn those Indians," Frank said. "And the half-breeds. We got 'em all over down where I'm from. They're supposed to stay on those reservations, but they're beginning to think they can go anywhere they damn well please."

"Just like blacks," agreed Stevens, his ironic tone completely missed by Frank.

"They're all ignorant sons-of-bitches, you ask me," Frank said, looking to me for confirmation. "Them and the gooks they got all over this country. ARVN, Viet Cong, it don't matter. They're all ignorant sons-of-bitches."

I made what I should have realized would be a futile effort to counter Frank's prejudices. "You know, Indians do a lot of the skilled labor on skyscrapers and tall structures, like the Arch. They can work at those heights without losing equilibrium."

"They just taking jobs away from real Americans. Put 'em back on the reservation, I say." He glared aggressively around the circle of faces, some of whom, I know, agreed with him. But Warren's presence, his intellectual strength, kept them silent.

"Middleton," Warren said. "You're right. There sure are some ignorant sons-of-bitches in the world."

Our little party broke up, and I never saw Stevens alive again. Frank had a month to live. And I would be haunted by each of them for decades.

XL

Frank Middleton. Warren Stevens. Anthony Roberts. These were the names I was now determined to find, even to touch, on the Vietnam Veterans Memorial in Washington. It was to be the culminating act in my series of confrontations with the past.

When I reported Ralph Banister's offer to Bella, I also announced that I was going to take this trip, a pilgrimage really, to the black granite wall that had at first divided and then united my fellow Vietnam veterans.

Her response was immediate and unqualified. "What a wonderful idea! I don't think I ever would have thought of it."

"All that talk I heard from Ralph inspired me," I explained. We were once more in our kitchen, a Sunday evening. "He wants to preserve a strip of old concrete for people to look at and be reminded of Route 66's place in American history. And I need somewhere specific to unload some . . . some sadness, some guilt, some memories. I've carried them inside long enough, and now maybe I can lay part of it down in an appropriate place."

"We all know how powerful a symbol it's been. Soldiers and relatives leave letters for their loved ones, flowers, personal tokens. It's healing, often a religious experience." She paused a moment. "Do you have something you'll take with you?"

"I do, several things, in fact. I don't plan to stop thinking about what happened after I've made this trip, though, or trying to learn from it. This isn't an end, only another stage. But I hope to be more at ease afterwards, to achieve a certain closure."

If I could find this sense of resolution, it had occurred to me, I might actually be of more use to others. As Ralph's consulting engineer, I'd be working in the future to celebrate America's strengths. And even in my Vietnam experience I now was realizing there had been courage and determination all around me--and even back at home--despite that war's being a confused campaign in the national mind. I shouldn't ignore, for instance, the nobility of Warren Stevens' tour.

Having been reminded by Ralph of the generations that preceded me, I decided what I would say to my children, the generation to come who so far had been spared major decisions of conscience in terms of national destiny. We would all sit down and talk, as I saw it. Even Nelson.

"Do you want me to go with you to Washington?" Bella asked, an almost pained expression on her face.

"Go with me?" I reached across the table to take her hand. "Of course! How could you think I would *not* want you?"

"This should be what you need; it's for you, the veteran."

"Oh, but one of the things I've learned in all this is that the folks at home had their crises of duty just like the troops did. I'm not sure I can ever forgive myself for not having been curious enough to learn about the Wash U. incident. I consider this trip . . . well, therapeutic for us both." She squeezed the hand that had taken hers.

And so, that spring, when the cherry blossoms were in full bloom on the mall of our national Capitol, Bella and I walked from a distant public parking lot across grassy plots to that famous black wall. I tried to focus on features of the memorial's construction, its materials and their arrangement.

In truth, I was worried that my composure might crumble when I got close to the wall, and I needed the engineer's view to help me put one foot in front of the other. What Bella was thinking as she walked, I

331

couldn't have said at the time, though now I have a pretty good idea.

She had added one stop to my Capitol visit, Washington's National Cathedral. She claimed it was for her, but she knew it mattered to me as well.

While we attended the service, she could well have been aware that, at the same time, Nelson was piling his personal belongings into the bed of Bill Pierce's pickup truck. He was moving back home from the Waites' apartment. Big Daddy's Road Hog, at one time the Midwest's next great rock band, had dissolved, less in dispute than in lost energy.

But it wasn't just the band's slowly coming apart that led to Nelson's return. Bella had been gently urging him toward that decision whenever she had the chance. If I'd been more alert, or a little less self-absorbed, I'd have realized he was coming by our house more often than his clothes needed washing.

To give myself some credit, I had pulled back from my initial desire to crash through the Waites' (garage) door and take my son back by force. (A goofy idea in more ways than one, as Nelson's force had exceeded mine for several years.) I also recognized I was in no frame of mind to talk rationally at that time. But years of marriage had taught me to count on Bella in such a situation--to act, or to tell me to act.

Talking to Bill, who had no child by either of his wives, had inspired me to one small gesture: a simple note written to Nelson at his garage apartment address. I told him he didn't need to live away from home to make his own decisions about the future. Music or college, he could count on my support.

Jenny, too, it turns out, was in on this plot to restore family order. She'd missed a brother to tease and be teased by--or perhaps she wanted a brother to blame, as she did when Taz escaped and nearly got flatted by Mrs. Thompson's minivan. Bella was also able to show Nelson that his uncertainty about the future was a factor in Jenny's pulling back from soccer and other school activities.

We'd all be in an uproar in another week about something, of course--embroidery supplies cluttering the den, loud music too late at night, required sit-down family meals, the new list of regular chores. But when Bella and I returned to St. Louis, we were a whole family again.

For some moments, I wondered if I could be whole in front of The Wall I'd come to touch. When I first saw it, from a distance of a hundred yards, the memorial was no more intimidating than its image on television. As we walked, however, I began to feel a lump rising in my throat and my breath went short.

A steady stream of people approached both outer ends of the two granite walls that connect at an angle of 125 degrees. We could see the slanted walks taking the group at each end down to the central meeting point.

The walls, each about 250 feet long, are low at each end, almost ground-level, so people seem to stand on top of the memorial. But at the central meeting point, the ground has been landscaped down so that the wall reaches above the visitors' heads to a height of ten feet. We could see people along both walks, most moving slowly down toward or away from the center, but a few were stopped at specific points.

I was relieved that we had to go first to a little booth some distance away from the wall for directions on how to proceed. The delay, I hoped, would allow me time to gather myself.

When I gave the names I was interested in, a park guide consulted his records and then produced three little slips of paper identifying the panels and the lines where I would find each name. Hand in hand, Bella and I joined the moving procession and took our journey together.

The names of those who died are arranged chronologically from the beginning of conflict to the American exit. At the low point of ground, weekly casualties were at their highest and the wall is tallest relative to the earth. As Bella and I walked, then, we went forward in time and down in elevation.

The Wall's position relative to the sun is deliberate, allowing light to bounce off the polished black granite and reflect shadowy images of the observers. Since the names are carved into the rock, you look deep into the memorial. But the memorial also throws you back out to yourself, to your own image on its surface.

Surely, I couldn't have done this any earlier! Images of Frank's aerial walk, sounds of Tony's talking about his imminent return to "The World," Warren's unsettling questions about our role in war would have come from nowhere and overwhelmed me.

Now, after everything I'd experienced in recent months, I could feel their lives blending into mine, their names from The Wall printed on my reflected face. I was made greater rather than lessened, and the poignancy of their history was deepened.

I put my hand on each name, tracing the letters and accepting their places among so many. At the foot of the panel where Tony's name was inscribed, I placed a copy of his audio tape. For Frank, a Matchbox bulldozer, once Nelson's. The hardest was Warren's. Near his name I put a cassette recorder's microphone, the cord trailing along the base of the wall.

For once, going uphill was easier than going down.

The End

Epilogue: Love After the Coral Court

This hot summer day belongs in mid-August, but we're halfway through September. Bella and I agree to meet after work at Ted Drewe's Frozen Custard for a cool dessert.

"You wear something--oh, I don't know--titillating," I suggest over the phone. For some reason, I've been more in the mood lately, despite our years.

"Titillating? You'll see racier outfits on the kids at Ted Drewe's than I'll wear in our bedroom!"

I laugh in agreement. High schoolers will be in their beach outfits on a day like this, and we are, after all, seriously middle-aged.

"Well, I can't propose a tryst at the Coral Court any more, you know." That Route 66 icon has been gone for several years, torn down and replaced by a nice, but undistinguished residential development. I'd been part of an effort to save the motel, but there wasn't sufficient backing to beat the developers. Later, the passage of the National Route 66 Historic Corridor Act might have given us more leverage, including Park Service support.

"Listen, Mark: you just try to avoid endangering your pension at the highway department today, and I'll endure a profoundly repetitive committee meeting. At home tonight, we'll find some way to amuse each other. After all, we have the house to ourselves."

Ah, how true! Nelson is at least closer than he's been for several years with his new post in Kansas City's Office of Urban Management, and Jenny is writing her dissertation in biochemistry at Cambridge. We don't even have (yet!) a new dog to terrorize us, after losing Taz at eighteen years of age. We bless e-mail every day for allowing us to stay close to our children.

Bella and I are not ready for retirement, but we've had those recommended meetings with financial advisers to lay out a plan that will get us there. Our calendars are full of the volunteer and leisure activity that will keep us busy when formal work comes to an end, probably in considerably less than a decade.

When I see Bella pull into Ted Drewe's, driving the latest in our string of family minivans, I also say a prayer of gratitude for our continuing good health. Oh, there have been complications over the years, but, thanks to modern medicine, we soldier on with regular exercise, sensible diet, proper medication.

I'd found a spot of shade to park in, so I'm leaning against the front fender of my PT Cruiser when Bella steps out to greet me. Buying that Cruiser is as close as I've come to indulging in a mid-life crisis. Bella admits it's a good deal short of the customary red convertible and trendy outfits. I give her the credit for keeping me sane, and old Ralph Banister, still kicking past age 90, for giving me a new purpose at just the right time.

"In this heat," I tell Bella, "any calories we take in will be sweated out, so I'm ordering whatever I want."

"I'm willing to pretend if you are. Let's say we each weigh the same as we did when we graduated from high school."

This evokes another merry laugh from each of us. While we're doing well for our age, any comparison of our broadened and settled bodies with the tanned and taut youth around us underscores how far we have traveled from younger selves.

"How was your day?" I ask the head of Counseling Services at St. Louis University.

"I'm earning my pay, let me assure you. Not, of course, when tangling with the bureaucracy. Thank goodness I still get to work with students."

We walk to the "Order Here" window, where we will have to stand in line for several minutes. Because this is the age of bare midriffs and low-riding shorts, bands of flesh appear in front of me, featuring tattoo butterflies, roses, serpents.

As I'm ordering two of Ted Drewe's famous Concretes, I test a tooth that Bill Pierce has been working on for the last year (not the one which Dr. Hartman saved with a root canal, but another molar). Bill is optimistic about the situation, but the third filling replacement he did a month ago already feels a bit loose.

"There's a real difference," Bella observes as we move toward the pickup line, "between these kids and my students."

"High school and college? Sure, they grow up. Though some of these kids have all they'll ever need in physical maturity."

"I can see that, too," Bella agrees, raising an eyebrow at a boy in tight T-shirt and tighter jeans stepping up to the adjacent window. Many of these kids work out. "They're fit in one way, but I worry about another."

We get our ice creams and look for a place to sit, but it's so crowded on this hot day we decide to stand in the shade leaning on my Cruiser.

Bella continues. "Up until September 11, a year ago, the generation I see at school had lived a charmed life. The last event that suggested anything might go wrong on their journey to good jobs and splendid homes was the Challenger accident. That shook up our national psyche, but it was in their infancies."

"I see what you mean. We had Kennedy's assassination, then Vietnam, Watergate, the whole mess."

"And the Civil Rights movement. I grew up with segregation in the South, and you were certainly close enough to read about events in Little Rock."

"Nowadays there's resistance even to that. Some talk of reverse discrimination."

"Still, whatever people's position, we all feel we can solve these problems--affirmative action, or an end to affirmative action. What I'm hearing my college students tell me involves forces outside the nation, the 'War on Terror.' They're beginning to realize that there's stuff out there that threatens us all."

"Now I see what you're getting at. I've thought about it, too. Today's youth is suddenly realizing they'll have to make some choices just as previous generations did. Where do we fight terrorists? At home or abroad? If abroad, where?"

With everyone else, I had worried about this after the attacks on the World Trade Center and the Pentagon, the field in Pennsylvania. America was going to need a lot of troops to control Iraq, North Korea-- what the politicians call "rogue states"--and terrorist organizations like Al Qaeda.

My first reaction, I'm embarrassed to admit, was selfish gratitude that my kids were probably too old to be required to serve. They were both past the age my generation had found to be the upper limit for the draft.

Nelson and Jenny, in fact, have been part of a very lucky generation: their parents rode the general economic boom of the '80s and 90's; they witnessed the fall of Communism and the end of the Cold War; U.S. military intervention was accomplished with high tech precision and almost no human casualties--on our side, of course.

"The ones who come in to talk," said Bella, "are not just worried about whether they'll have to serve. They're beginning to question our obligation, as the richest country in the world, to others less fortunate. As the world's only superpower, we can just about do what we want. But what should we do?"

There it is. Our national road had been smooth for another generation's childhood. It was like Route 66 reaching perfection: efficient, high-speed travel to all destinations, but still preserving a sense of national community in Mom-and-Pop restaurants, locally owned motels, and compelling roadside attractions. Then came the interstate and ubiquitous, identical franchises. All places turned into one place.

We'd even imagined, I think, that our way of life would spread around the globe, the American Dream ready for all other peoples. Traveling America's Main Street to Vietnam, I'd learned that no such journey would be as easy or as simple as predicted.

342

Other peoples, with different pasts, choose other roads to travel.

"Look at them," I say, amused by a group of giggling teenagers gathered around a bright red pickup truck with oversize cab and giant, blocked wheels. The truck's music system is loud, but not excessively so, except perhaps the bass that thumps *boom-ba-ba-boom* beneath the tune and inspires one especially attractive girl to move her hips in rhythmic accentuation.

"They are the future," Bella says. The crowd is a delightful model of contemporary diversity, including, I'm reasonably sure, at least one Vietnamese-American.

When I took my pilgrimage to the Vietnam Veterans Memorial, I pretended that my life's great, unwanted challenge was at last behind me. Future wars were the responsibility of others, like these children entertaining themselves right in front of me. I would let them shape the country of their children.

"I think," I tell Bella. "I think you've just proposed a discussion topic for the church youth group. I'll call Bill tonight about our next meeting."

The end

Route 66 books by Michael Lund

Growing Up on Route 66 — Michael Lund (2000) ISBN 1-888725-31-1 Novel evoking fond memories of what it was like to grow up alongside "America's Highway" in 20th Century Missouri. (Trade paperback) 5x8 260 pp

Route 66 Kids — Michael Lund (2002) ISBN 1-888725-70-2 Sequel to *Growing Up on Route 66*, continuing memories of what it was like to grow up alongside "America's Highway" in 20th Century Missouri. (Trade paperback) 5x8 270 pp

A Left-hander on Route 66--Michael Lund (2003) ISBN 1-888725-88-5. Twenty years after the fact, left-hander Hugh Noone appeals a wrongful conviction that detoured him from "America's Main Street" and put him in jail. But revealing the details of the past and effecting a resolution of his case mean a dramatic rearrangement of his world, including troubled relationships with three women: Linda Roy, Patty Simpson, and Karen Murphy. (Trade paperback) 5x8 270 pp

Route 66 Spring-- Michael Lund (2004) ISBN: 1-888725-98-2. The lives of four young Missourians are changed when a bottle comes to the surface of one of the state's many natural springs. Inside is a letter written by a girl a dozen years after the end of the Civil War. Lucy Rivers Johns ' epistle contains a sad story of family failure and a powerful plea for help. This message from the last century crystallizes the individual frustrations of Janet Masters, Freddy Sills, Louis Clark, and Roberta Green, another group of Route 66 kids. Their response to the past charts a bold path into the future, a path inspired by the Mother Road itself. (Trade paperback) 5x8 270 pp.

Miss Route 66--Michael Lund (2004) ISBN 1-888725-96-6. In the fourth novel of Michael Lund's Route 66 Novel Series, Susan Bell tells the story of her candidacy in Fairfield, Missouri's annual beauty contest. Now married and with teenage children in St. Louis, she recounts her youthful adventure in this small town along "America's Highway." At the same time, she plans a return to Fairfield in order to right injustices she feels were done to some young contestants in the Miss Route 66 Pageant. (Trade paperback) 5½ X8¼, 260 pp, **Audiobook** on 5 CD's ISBN 1-888725-12-5

Route 66 to Vietnam Michael Lund (2004) ISBN 1-59630-000-0 This novel takes characters from earlier works in the Route 66 Novel Series farther west than Los Angeles, official destination of the famous highway,

Route 66. Mark Landon and Billy Rhodes find the values they grew up on challenged by America's role in Southeast Asia. But elements of their upbringing represented by the Mother Road also sustain them in ways they could never have anticipated. . (Trade paperback) 5½ X8¼, 270 pp

AudioBook on CD — Route 66 to Vietnam ISBN: 1-59630-011-6 Michael Lund's fictional commentary from the viewpoint of a draftee. by Michael Lund unabridged 6 CD's --9 hours running time.

Route 66 Chapel Michael Lund (2006) ISBN 1-59630-012-4 Route 66 Chapel, Michael Lund (2006) (Trade paperback) 5½ X8¼, 260 pp,. When the forces of progress threaten the foundation of smalltown life — a small church — five senior citizens, a mysterious newcomer, and one young couple band together in an unlikely campaign to save it. The embattled meeting point of old and new is Route 66 Chapel, a building curiously linked to America's "Mother Road."

Route 66 Choir-- A Comedy (2010)

Michael Lund ISBN 9781596300583   284 pp 5" x 8   In Route 66 Choir Stanley Measure takes early retirement just before September 11, 2001, and his impulsive decisions participate in an unraveling of confidence in the American way of life. His wife Felicia finds that everything she holds dear is in danger of coming apart: her marriage, her church, her business, and even her country. Who or what can orchestrate the recovery of harmony necessary to sustain the spirit of the Mother Road?

Route 66 Bride (Fall 2010)

BeachHouse Books

www.beachhousebooks.com

(636) 394-4950

an Imprint of
𝕾cience & 𝕳umanities 𝕻ress
PO Box 7151
Chesterfield, MO
63006-7151